LOVE'S TREASURE

Sunset SEALs Book 7

SHARON HAMILTON

SHARON HAMILTON'S BOOK LIST

SEAL BROTHERHOOD BOOKS

SEAL BROTHERHOOD SERIES
Accidental SEAL Book 1
Fallen SEAL Legacy Book 2
SEAL Under Covers Book 3
SEAL The Deal Book 4
Cruisin' For A SEAL Book 5
SEAL My Destiny Book 6
SEAL of My Heart Book 7
Fredo's Dream Book 8
SEAL My Love Book 9
SEAL Encounter Prequel to Book 1
SEAL Endeavor Prequel to Book 2
Ultimate SEAL Collection Vol. 1 Books 1-4 /2 Prequels
Ultimate SEAL Collection Vol. 2 Books 5-7

SEAL BROTHERHOOD LEGACY SERIES
Watery Grave Book 1
Honor The Fallen Book 2
Grave Injustice Book 3

BAD BOYS OF SEAL TEAM 3 SERIES
SEAL's Promise Book 1
SEAL My Home Book 2

SEAL's Code Book 3
Big Bad Boys Bundle Books 1-3

BAND OF BACHELORS SERIES
Lucas Book 1
Alex Book 2
Jake Book 3
Jake 2 Book 4
Big Band of Bachelors Bundle

BONE FROG BROTHERHOOD SERIES
New Year's SEAL Dream Book 1
SEALed At The Altar Book 2
SEALed Forever Book 3
SEAL's Rescue Book 4
SEALed Protection Book 5
Bone Frog Brotherhood Superbundle

BONE FROG BACHELOR SERIES
Bone Frog Bachelor Book 0.5
Unleashed Book 1
Restored Book 2

SUNSET SEALS SERIES
SEALed at Sunset Book 1
Second Chance SEAL Book 2
Treasure Island SEAL Book 3
Escape to Sunset Book 4
The House at Sunset Beach Book 5

Second Chance Reunion Book 6
Love's Treasure Book 7
Finding Home Book 8 (releasing summer 2022)
Sunset SEALs Duet #1
Sunset SEALs Duet #2

LOVE VIXEN
Bone Frog Love

SHADOW SEALS
Shadow of the Heart

SILVER SEALS SERIES
SEAL Love's Legacy

SLEEPER SEALS SERIES
Bachelor SEAL

STAND ALONE BOOKS & SERIES
SEAL's Goal: The Beautiful Game
Nashville SEAL: Jameson
True Blue SEALS Zak
Paradise: In Search of Love
Love Me Tender, Love You Hard

NOVELLAS
SEAL You In My Dreams Magnolias and Moonshine

PARANORMALS

GOLDEN VAMPIRES OF TUSCANY SERIES
Honeymoon Bite Book 1
Mortal Bite Book 2
Christmas Bite Book 3
Midnight Bite Book 4

THE GUARDIANS
Heavenly Lover Book 1
Underworld Lover Book 2
Underworld Queen Book 3
Redemption Book 4

FALL FROM GRACE SERIES
Gideon: Heavenly Fall

NOVELLAS
SEAL Of Time Trident Legacy

All of Sharon's books are available on Audible, narrated by the talented J.D. Hart.

Copyright © 2022 by Sharon Hamilton
Print Edition

All rights reserved. Without limiting the rights under copyright reserved above, no part of this publication may be reproduced, stored in or introduced into a retrieval system, or transmitted, in any form, or by any means (electronic, mechanical, photocopying, recording, or otherwise) without the prior written permission of the copyright owner of this book.

This is a work of fiction. Names, characters, places, brands, media, and incidents are either the product of the author's imagination or are used fictitiously. In many cases, liberties and intentional inaccuracies have been taken with rank, description of duties, locations and aspects of the SEAL community.

ABOUT THE BOOK

Love Blooms. Danger Looms.

One year has passed since Navy SEAL Ned Silver found the love of his life, his mermaid, Madison, in the beautiful waters of Florida's Gulf Coast. The two of them have embarked on two great adventures: a love affair worthy of Poseidon himself, and a thrilling underwater discovery of a long-lost Spanish Galleon possibly worth millions.

As they explore the depths of their relationship, frolicking in the warm waters littered with ghosts of dreams lost and shipwrecks abundant, dangerous secrets are revealed. Ned wonders if being a Navy SEAL really is his higher calling, or is he now being drawn to remain at Madison's side in Florida, giving up the Coronado lifestyle and his buddies on Team 3. Just as his father did some twenty plus years ago, Ned has found love and adventure to fill a lifetime, and a treasure more valuable than gold or silver, to protect…

If he can fight his way to the finish line.

AUTHOR'S NOTE

This is dedicated to all those who have loved once, twice, perhaps three times or more, and thought they should give up. I believe in Happily Ever Afters. I believe in long slow kisses and moonlit strolls on the beach. I believe in walks in the woods on sunny days. I believe in forgiveness and the healing power of true love.

Love hurts and makes us strong at the same time. I believe it brings us to the truest expression of ourselves, and when we strive for true love, we are striving for the very best within our souls.

Yes, even for Navy SEALs, ***True Love Heals in the Gardens of the Heart.***

No, not everyone gets an HEA. No, not every relationship can be saved, just as not every life can be spared when found in harm's way. But in my books, I try to show what could happen. And yes, I know the difference between reality and fiction, but I also know where I like to live.

Live well and love often. And let's explore the depths our hearts can take us, even in this very short ride of life.

—Sharon Hamilton

I support two main charities. Navy SEAL/UDT Museum operates in Ft. Pierce, Florida. Please learn about this wonderful museum, all run by active and former SEALs and their friends and families, and who rely on public support, not that of the U.S. Government.
www.navysealmuseum.org

I also support Wounded Warriors, who tirelessly bring together the warrior as well as the family members who are just learning to deal with their soldier's condition and have nowhere to turn. It is a long path to becoming well, but I've seen first-hand what this organization does for its warriors and the families who love them. Please give what your heart tells you is right. If you cannot give, volunteer at one of the many service centers all over the United States. Get involved. Do something meaningful for someone who gave so much of themselves, to families who have paid the price for your freedom. You'll find a family there unlike any other on the planet.
www.woundedwarriorproject.org

CHAPTER 1

NED SILVER AND the rest of his SEAL Team 3 buddies were unceremoniously dumped at the Coronado airport by a military-contracted flight. A group of women, parents, and children welcomed them just outside the chain-link fence near the visitors' reception area. The team had just returned from a short trip to Baja California. Hugs, giggles, and some tears were shed by the audience present to welcome their homecoming heroes. The team had only been gone three months, but that didn't interfere with the ardor or exuberance of their greetings.

None of them were there for Ned.

He slapped backs of some of his teammates, slung his duty bag over his right shoulder, waved at several faces in the greeting party he knew, passed by the rest of the family grouping, and gave a salute to two Lieutenant Commanders and their team handler. Then it was off to the parking lot to climb into his Hummer and crash at his condo with the tiny slice of ocean view so small he could measure it in inches.

He planned to call Madison, who was probably waiting tables and tending bar at the Salty Dog, but he wanted to organize his thoughts first.

His emotional state was flat. Not that he didn't *feel* things, but he just didn't have the energy to react to them. He didn't talk. He didn't smile. He didn't stare, and he'd tried to sleep during the bumpy flight from Cabo to Coronado but gave up unsuccessfully, turning it into a jostling, noisy meditation even his ear buds and Two Steps From Hell cranked up to nearly max volume couldn't drown out. Only good thing about it was that the noise made conversation impossible, while his closed eyes signaled he didn't want anyone to try.

As Ned approached the Hummer and climbed inside, he carefully pulled out his cell phone. Staring down at the dial face, he wondered if Madison would be able to hear his ring over the din of the usual noise on a Friday night at the Salty Dog. He imagined there would be live music, and the place would be packed, most customers looking for the snow crab special and happy hour pricing.

She picked up on the first ring.

"I got a little vibration on my fanny and could just tell it was you. So when the heck are you getting out here to Florida? I need you. How about driving for four days straight?" she asked in her fresh voice.

It was such a relief to hear her while he was standing on US soil.

"You can tell it's my call just by the way it tickles your fanny? Is that what you're saying?"

"Something like that. There's more to that story of course. But you'll have to stand in front of me naked before you're gonna hear it. I'm just wondering when that's going to happen."

"If you close your eyes, we could do it now. But if you want the real thing, I was planning on flying out tomorrow morning. I kind of need to sleep off some crummy shit, Madison. These deployments to Mexico never get any better. I wonder what the heck we're doing there. But I'm home, and that's all that matters."

She went cold stone quiet. He heard clanging in the background—dishes and their Cajun cook dressing down some poor kitchen help.

"Did I scare you off, Maddie?" he asked, thinking he might have offended her in some way.

"Not possible. Just thinking about you being here tomorrow has my panties soaking wet."

"I love the sound of that, sweetheart."

She paused, gave him an enormous sigh, and added, "Gotta distract myself with customers. Love hearing your voice, Ned. Can't wait until tomorrow. We've got a lot to talk about. And, of course, I'm requesting the use of your naked body, as much as you are up to, that is."

He chuckled. He like that. "You know, I was kind of tired, but if you'd promise to talk to me the whole way, I might be able to drive straight through. What would it be? Forty-eight hours?"

He knew it didn't make sense but was all he could muster.

"I like the idea of you snuggling in your own bed tonight, getting all of those restorative juices back up and running and anticipating being here tomorrow. Oh, I almost forgot—bring some extra gear, Ned, if you have anything fancy to play with. Noonan's got a big new dive coming up, and we have to go deeper to get it." She ended her sentence with a sultry whisper.

"I like deeper."

"Yes. You. Do. And so do I. But any little extra gadgets or dive prototypes your bosses are testing might be helpful in this circumstance. And that's all I'm going to say. Night, sailor boy."

She signed off with a kiss, and now Ned was going to have to battle his hard-on all the way to his condo.

Madison had been the only woman he'd fallen head-over-heels for at first glance. Ned had never believed in such a phenomenon before he met her. She was all the right kind of long and lean in all the perfect places, muscular and strong where she needed to be.

He lay awake at night thinking about what she looked like swimming above him, with her darned pink flippers and the skin-tight wetsuit that accentuated her curves. Her blonde hair was usually tied in a long braid during dives, but he'd seen it floating all around her head like a golden cloud. She was the perfect vision of the perfect woman who Ned didn't have any right to claim for his own. But he was so glad that he did.

But the best part was she made him feel like Triton or Poseidon himself on his golden throne when she was beside him. She brought out all the best parts of him, and she kissed away and bandaged up his many flaws. He felt braver, more relaxed, and happier than he'd ever been before. He prayed they'd have time to explore and make this relationship into something lasting. That was his goal this visit—to build on what they'd started and make it permanent.

But just as fast as her vision appeared, it disappeared, and his chest filled with some dark foreboding left over from a difficult mission in Mexico. And they were all getting hard—each one worse than the next. Something had been eating away at the Team. Everything seemed to be off-kilter, out of sync. There were fights amongst the men—small disagreements at work irritating him. He found he didn't have the patience to deal with the group dynamics. He began to wonder if he still fit in.

Has it come to that?

One of the things he had learned from the older team guys, including Kyle, was that the time to get out was when it wasn't fun anymore. Was it now a challenge because he wanted to do different things with his life since meeting Madison? He'd put in a good ten years. He had an exemplary record and was told he'd be up for promotion soon, if he wanted it. Kyle had encouraged him to go to OCS. But Ned wasn't sure the Navy was his real future any longer. He'd enjoyed it, but less now. Perhaps the end of the road had come.

Ned worried what Madison would think or whether he should even tell her until he was sure. They'd made plans to be together after this last deployment, and that spark was still there he'd missed these past two months. But there hadn't been a formal commitment made. It was loosely assumed. That's the way most of Ned's life had been run.

He was conflicted. With this new relationship, his life was more complicated.

Am I really ready for this? Is this what I really want? Am I making the right decision in waiting, or should I just say "fuck it" and do it?

He felt like he was in two places at the same time. He let his mind wander all the way home.

Would Madison be in favor of him leaving the teams? Or would she distrust a decision abandoning a good paying job, leadership potential, and a real chance in a permanent career for the life of a beach bum, perhaps helping her tend the Salty Dog? Yes, they might run into some serious cash with his treasure dive. But that wasn't a sure thing. And he wanted a sure thing before he made that life commitment to Madison.

The story of the old barge that sank off the Florida coast, along with hundreds of other ships that had also perished there over time, piqued his thirst for adventure and love of history. They'd been contracted by a family to find a missing artifact, a dog collar, which had sentimental value to the family and belonged to the cook's dog, Otis. In that story was an old romance, a story of love lost. Of course, with the backdrop of the Civil War brewing and the age of piracy having just passed its heyday, it was already full of intrigue and danger. But adding the fact that they found a Spanish Galleon during their search made it an even greater story. He'd been called up on deployment without having his rightfully earned time to do the exploration and had missed out on some of the adventure.

If Madison was correct, maybe old Noonan had discovered something else. It was always possible. But his visit back to Florida didn't have anything to do with buried treasure. It was really all about Madison. She was the real treasure in his life.

He laid everything out on his bed, packed and unpacked several shirts, shorts, and all his flip-flops. He really didn't have much left, except for the bolted armory box in his closet. It would not be possible to bring all his weapons since he was going to fly. Perhaps he could talk one of the other SEALs he met in Florida to drive them out for him. But that was a small problem. A minuscule problem at that.

You shouldn't be concerned about little things, Ned. Only the big stuff counts.

He walked through his apartment one more time after he showered, put on his pajama bottoms, stared at the bare walls—still empty since he never had time to decorate and never entertained. There was a definite look of a bachelor pad here; no trace of a woman existed. Even a used nighty or some underwear would make him feel better, but it just wasn't there. This was not where his love was, where he wanted to be, where he needed to be to survive. This was the place he crashed, restored himself in between deployments, and hoped the rest of his life showed up.

He placed his final choices inside his duffel bag, including a few pieces of gear he picked up at one of the scuba dive shows he'd attended in San Diego, the book of poetry his mother had given him, a few pictures of her and his dad, and a handful of things from his childhood in a small box, and zipped the whole package up.

It felt like he was never coming back, or perhaps the man who would walk in the door the next time would be different than the man standing here now. Whichever way it flowed, he was just going to go with it, see where his heart took him, and let fate and the mermaid take hold of his hand and lead him down that blue watery path.

BEFORE TURNING IN, he called his mother.

"Oh, Ned, I'm so happy you're safe and going back out there again. I had such a lovely time. I just keep seeing those beautiful sunsets, that white beach, Madison's mother's colorful paintings in the house, her caftan, and all her eclectic friends. I felt like I was twenty years old."

"I noticed. And I'm glad. I think you should fly out there again."

"Well, your aunt is adjusting quite well, and with each passing week, she seems to recognize me less and less, so there is that possibility now, but I'll visit more often. Amberley has invited me to stay with her if I want it. It would just be temporary."

Ned was glad to hear the happiness in her voice. She was beginning to explore outside her small world in San Diego after Ned's father's death. It was a healthy sign.

"I think that's a fine idea."

"Really? You really do?"

"I know I was quite harsh with you the first time I saw you there. It was a shock. No one told me you were coming. But after I saw how everyone fit in, I realized I was just the last one to except what everyone else already knew."

"I was not happy with how that happened. But I'm glad you found your peace with it. I don't think there was any other way that it would've worked for me, except to just jump in. You know, dive in headfirst like you do."

"No, we don't dive in headfirst, Mom. We jump in with our flippers first. We sort of slip into the water seat. That's the way we do it. You dive in headfirst and, all of a sudden, you've lost all your gear."

His mother laughed. It was great to hear the mirth in her voice.

"Oh, Ned, I think the way you describe things is marvelous. Of course, it would be me who would think about jumping in head first. I've always been risk averse."

"Not so, Mom. Remember, you married old Jake, the pirate. That was a leap of faith if ever I heard one."

She chuckled. "Now you've made me spit out my tea!"

They ended their call with a promise to meet up in

Florida again in a few weeks' time. Ned let his mother know that he was considering leaving the Navy. She was cautious in her response but said she trusted him.

Ned wasn't sure he could trust himself.

Before retiring, he checked his voicemail and chose to listen to Noonan's message, since Madison had already spilled the beans.

"I'll be picking you up in Tampa. But I just couldn't wait. Ned, this is the call I always wanted to make to your dad. But now I have the honor to give it to you instead. We're going to be fucking rich, my boy! And Otis's collar led me right to it!"

CHAPTER 2

THE AIRPORT WAS as busy as it always was. San Diego, a huge military hub, was dotted with uniforms of all branches. Wives, husbands, and loved ones greeted soldiers coming home, including an occasional honor guard standing to attention to receive coffins sadly returning. Young men and women said their goodbyes to young brides, husbands, and children. Pregnant wives and children waited impatiently for the sight of that one special person to come bounding down the corridors of the airport and into their arms. Young women, also in fatigues, said goodbye to their children and families, arms wrapped around each other in groups of two or three, heading off to an occupation somewhere. Ned saw these service men and women as members of his tribe, and he was honored to be counted among them.

He was offered a first-class upgrade because of his military ID and sat next to an attractive young woman heading back to Dallas and her home nearby. He always loved listening to Texas accents, especially on women. She was about ten years his senior, very well educated, and delightful to sit next to. She was well-versed in many subjects—especially travel and world affairs—and had a nice manner without being overly opinionated. He like that. There were a lot of things ruminating inside him he wasn't sure he was ready to open a discussion about.

"What do you do in Dallas, if I may ask?" He wasn't sure it was the right thing to do, but she'd been very pleasant and didn't ask him a single question. She'd made comments about his tats and suggested she knew he had a dangerous job. He liked that too. It made him trust her, even if just a little bit. She wasn't pushy.

The question elicited a measured smile, more like a smirk, followed by a sigh as she rolled her eyes. He knew he wasn't going to like what she had to say next.

"Actually, I'm a psychologist. I pegged you for a military man, because I work with a lot of vets. Sadly, I work in suicide prevention."

Her sparkly green eyes studied him carefully as he decided what face to show her. This was uncharted waters.

"Wow. I tip my cap to you, ma'am. I'm not sure I could do that. I mean, I'm there for my buddies, people

I know, but I'm not sure I could ever do that for strangers. But you're right. It is a problem. And I'm glad you're addressing it."

"You know, I find that most of the really tragic suicides are not people that run around all crazy and freaked out all the time. That's not a psych or medical term, by the way. It's a favorite term of my mothers, from her hippy days." She smiled, which disarmed him. Finding words all of a sudden became awkward.

"I use freaked out a lot. On the Teams." Ned immediately wished he could take those words back and realized he had breached the wall he meant to avoid. He hadn't wanted to tell her he was a SEAL. But he continued anyway.

"Oops, my loose tongue gave myself away, I guess. I'm with a Team at Coronado."

"I was just there, working with a group of Navy recruits, giving a couple of lectures. I also was contracted to do some assessments of a unit that suffered heavy casualties in a rescue operation. I believe some of your SEAL brothers were in that operation, if I could be so bold as to say that."

He knew about the tragic rescue operation where half of SEAL Team 5 Charlie platoon was gunned down in an ambush in West Africa. It was not part of the globe he looked forward to going back to anytime soon. Mexico was almost as bad to him.

"You're talking about the guys on SEAL Team 5?"

She nodded, a tiny frown line exposed between her eyebrows. "As I said, most of the damage happens internally. You guys are trained to hide it. And you must, in combat situations. I know platoon leaders who suffer nightmares for twenty years or more afterwards, when they lose guys or even have guys that are injured or permanently disabled. Choosing who to send and who to keep back has to be done in a non-emotional way. However, the results can wind up causing an extreme emotional reaction."

Ned looked straight ahead, not willing to reveal anything of that emotional side. He'd seen one man fall in his ten years as a SEAL and heard about others, people he knew, guys he really liked. Even a couple of assholes got wounded, and he still felt sorry for them.

But he wasn't going to be confide any of this. It just wasn't right, wasn't something he felt he could reveal to someone, no matter how professional they appeared, how reasonable they were, even if it might benefit him or bring some comfort. He'd remain tough, even though he knew that was bullshit.

She must have sensed she'd hit a nerve. She quietly removed herself from the conversation and returned to her magazine. Ned was relieved.

When they landed in Dallas, she slipped him her card and promised that she would return the phone call if ever he wanted to chat or ask questions about her work. She always considered her work with individual vets, especially the elite core, to be just service done *gratis.*

"It was very nice to talk to you. I enjoyed it," he lied. "And now I realize I don't even know your name." Ned scanned her business card and tried, "Sherine?"

"That's the name my mother gave me. I don't necessarily like it, but I'm sticking with it." She extended her hand. "You have yourself a nice weekend, Sailor. I hope you don't miss your next flight. Dallas/Fort Worth is known for plucking people from their dreamy vacations and making them spend it in an uncomfortable chair for hours, sometimes all night. If that starts to happen,"—she leaned over and whispered softly—"let them get you a room. That's the least they could do." After they shook hands, she added, "Thank you for your service, and I know that's trite, but I mean it. You're one of the good guys."

Before he could answer, she was halfway down the hallway. The view of her graceful frame moving down the corridor towards baggage claim and the tram was not unpleasant.

Ned checked the gate for his connecting flight to Tampa and headed the opposite direction. He tucked her business card into his wallet and began to anticipate seeing Madison.

Hours later, his connecting plane took a hard landing, like one of those monster transports he was used to. It caused some of the overheads to spill their contents on the vulnerable passengers below. Ned assisted getting the bags safely stowed away, lending a hand to the attendants, even though the plane was still making its way down the runway to the gate.

The instant Ned walked from the downstairs baggage claim to the outside pickup area, the warm Florida evening caressing him all over, he was suddenly filled with joy. This was the place he belonged now. He chuckled that he'd been so nervous. But now he knew, this was it. It almost didn't matter what Madison said. He wanted to spend the rest of his life here.

The pirate was there to pick him up as had been previously arranged. The old man ran with a limp and nearly body slammed Ned, which was borderline humiliating. The crusty friend of his recently passed father was difficult to shake.

As Ned tried to extricate himself, the pirate kept his right arm around his neck and whispered in his ear, "Ned, my boy. Hope you got my message. We're going to be so stinkin' rich you'll get tired of spending all the money. I wish your father were alive to experience it all. But we've hit the mother lode!"

CHAPTER 3

MADISON KEPT CHECKING her cell phone, waiting for the call from Ned informing her that he had arrived. The Salty Dog was chock-full of snowbirds this evening, people who were fleeing the bad weather of the Northeast, Midwest, and even wildfires in California and Oregon.

She was training another new girl but kept an eye on a second bartender the owner had added. She suspected him of stealing from the till. She knew it was a common occurrence for bartenders, but that didn't make it right. It cheated everyone, and she had no patience for it.

Her mother was dressed in what she called her "highbrow hippie attire", the look she probably wore in her twenties. Now in her mid-fifties, Amberley's long, gray flowing curls and all the bright colors she could muster made her just as disarming as a twenty-something walking through the Salty Dog in a bikini.

She probably did that too.

But that was her mother—always looking to cause a stir, a lasting impression, impossible not to forgive when she erred, and double impossible not to laugh with. In fact, Madison hadn't met a single person who could be considered her enemy. Amberley got along with everyone.

The entertainment this evening was a pair of young songwriters, each wearing guitars that looked too big for their small frames. But their voices were very melodic, and although it was nothing you could dance to, the music was all original and very good. The crowd wasn't going to allow it to dampen their mood. The duo might as well have been screeching out soul music, the crowd was so enthusiastic.

She felt her phone flutter it in her back pocket.

"So you're here!" she squealed.

"In the flesh, Madison. Surviving another raucous ride with the pirate, who doesn't drive as good as he pilots a boat. But I don't think he's drunk."

In the background, Madison you could hear old Noonan La Fontaine's voice barking, "Not yet at least!"

"Well, just tell him to slow down, because I have plans for you, and it will be greatly interfered with if you're all bruised and bloodied. Tell him to get you here in one piece."

"Yes, ma'am."

Madison signed off quickly after noticing a fight developing at the end of the bar between two seventy-year-old men fighting over the same white-haired woman.

A couple of the owners' security guards were able to lend a hand, but the two men were quite difficult to separate. It was enhancing the entertainment value of the whole place. The police were called, and the two were removed from the premises, leaving the woman to fend for herself.

Madison approached her, considering offering assistance. "I guess nobody asked you if you have a way home?" she asked the frightened woman.

"I've got Carl's set of keys, luckily. But I don't have his house key. I guess I'll be spending the night in a motel."

"I certainly hope this sort of thing doesn't happen all the time. Are these guys friends?"

"Funny you should say that," the woman answered. "They're actually brothers. My mistake for dating both of them and marrying one of them very briefly. None of us expected to meet up again in Florida, but as they say, things happen in the Gulf. I was not prepared for this."

The woman straightened her dress, took down her hair and re-clipped it up at the top of her head again. Madison had an idea.

"Do you see that attractive woman over there sitting with several people at that table?"

The woman nodded quickly.

"Her name is Amberley, and she's my mother. She's usually a great shoulder to cry on, knows all the eligible locals, and is a great friend. She collects people like stray cats and turns them into prized possessions."

"She's your mother, you say?"

"Unbelievable, right?"

"Now that you tell me, the two of you actually look quite a lot alike. I'm sorry I didn't see the resemblance. You are sure she'd be okay with a stranger crashing her little foursome?"

"The more the merrier. She'll tell you the same thing if you ask her."

Madison followed the woman as she introduced herself to her mother and three others seated at the table, all men. One guy stood, bowed slightly, and brought a chair for her. That made the odds shift a bit, two women for three men. Madison figured that was about right.

Ned's rock-solid frame sauntered in through the double doors open to the night air. The sight of him always gave her butterflies and sucked the wind right out of her. His lithe body, with muscles that could fill out a pair of jeans very well, made a beeline for her with a gait and swagger that only a tall man could afford. He stared right at her, and her heart skipped a couple of beats as he crossed the hushed room.

"Well, look what old Noonan dragged in this evening."

He stepped up on the bar rail, leaned over, grabbed her face in his huge hands, and planted a deep, wet kiss on her lips. "Miss me?"

Madison loved the way he made her swoon. "Of course. More than breathing. More than life itself. So how was it?"

This tour in Mexico had been unlike several others the Team had taken, and Madison wasn't quite sure what they'd run into, but Ned had never been on a deployment, short or long, where he didn't call home every day. Yet for this one, she had to do most of the calling or she suspected she wouldn't have spoken to him at all.

Ned's expression went dark. He was good at drawing out the face armor, that part of him that was so difficult to read, especially when his mouth smiled but his eyes look dead. He was trying very hard to look cheerful, but she knew something was wrong.

"It went okay. I'm glad it's over. And that's all I wanna say tonight, if you don't mind." Ned was very clear in dishing out ground rules. Madison didn't want to risk crossing any of those lines. He'd talk about it when he was good and ready, and not before then.

"Hey, Ned, this is me. This is paradise, your home," she reminded him.

That did the trick. He rewarded her with a broad smile.

"Any chance you could get off early?" he asked.

"Not much. But if you want, you can take my car. I'll catch a ride home with one of the other girls. You can shower, unpack—maybe walk the beach a bit until I'm done here. We are a bit short-staffed tonight, as always. We've already put down one fight, and I'm hoping the crowd will settle down a bit. I'm cutting off a few people, requesting a couple get a taxi and go home, and pretty soon will stop taking orders for dinner."

"Nope." Now he was dancing with that playfulness she loved. "I'm going to sit right over there near your mother, eavesdrop, and watch you scrub down those counters, bend over to pick up beer bottles, and lean over the counter with that very awesome but way too small T-shirt you've got on there."

"So I'll consider myself monitored then, is that right?"

"Abso-fuckin-lutely."

It had been over two months since Ned's arms had encircled her waist, since she'd experienced how artfully, delicately he undressed her, playing her body like a finely-tuned violin. Whatever darkness or questions she had about his demeanor were completely obliterated as they took their time, got reacquainted, and connected both spiritually and physically. He lovingly shattered all her fears except one.

She'd be desperate without him.

She told herself over again that these weeks of separation were things she had to get used to, that it wouldn't interfere with her happiness, her daily life. Now, in Ned's arms, she felt like he had brought her back to life—resuscitated after a long sleep under water. The magic of their love overcame the impossible odds. She'd been so wrong about this. And just like all the other times he'd been deployed, the leaving was getting more and more difficult. She suspected that this one would hurt more than the rest but tried to convince herself otherwise. Now she understood.

She'd been wrong.

They didn't make it home for hours. After they made love, he lay back against the pillow, watching the moon darting behind large white clouds on the horizon. Madison placed her cheek over his left upper rib cage, rubbing her hand up and down the ripples of his abs. She felt safe, secure, and never wanted to leave his side.

Seconds later, Otis jumped up on the bed and attempted to bury himself in the soft covers between them, making little squeaky moans that had them both giggling.

"Why, you little rascal. Look at you!" Ned laughed.

As if embarrassed by his own boldness, Otis ducked his head beneath a flap of sheet beneath Madison's upper chest.

"He's my constant companion. After you left, he made the adjustment easily coming over to my place. I don't think he'd hurt anyone, but he's a heck of a watch dog," she added. In babytalk, she whispered, "We were good for each other, weren't we, Otis?"

The dog lifted his head, stared back and forth between the two of them, and then attempted to bury himself again in the covers.

"I'm surprised he didn't bark at me. I've been gone so long in this dog's life."

"I think he's a keeper, Ned. I leave him inside now most the time, only let him out for brief potty breaks or when he sees something he wants to chase. Have to be careful though, or I'll be running down the beach while Otis is in search of a pelican or egret."

"We'll take him to the dog park later, after I figure out what's going on here. Glad you're taking care of my girl, Otis." he said as he scratched the top of the dog's head around his ears.

The dog accepted the praise and, as if working on a checklist in his head, jumped off the bed to pursue something else in the house.

"Independent, too," Ned commented.

"Very. Still a little unpredictable but loyal. I think he's grateful after being a street dog for who knows how long. I'm glad you befriended him."

She adjusted herself against Ned's hard body, which was sweating like a turbine, blood infusing into his muscles and regulating his heartbeat, which had gone from racing to nearly normal, just like hers. She knew he had questions for her.

So did she.

"Tell me about this new dive of Noonan's. He was all excited about striking it rich, and I practically had to put duct tape over him in the airport for fear of him telling everybody at the baggage claim about it," Ned chuckled.

"That's Noonan. Except this time, I think he really has found something. He wanted to wait until you came before he explained it to both of us. He just couldn't hold it any longer. But yes, he thinks we're all going to be buying houses on the beach. Can you believe it?"

"I guess if he hadn't been such a good friend of my father's, I might believe him more. I don't think he's conning us, Madison. I just wish he'd be a little more discreet about it. And he normally is. I hope he's got it all locked up this time." Ned's eyes stared from under worried brow lines.

"After the first dive, when we had to fend off those jerks who tried to take it all away, I would've thought the old captain would be a little more careful. So I think you're right, Ned. We better talk to him right away and make sure he doesn't blow it for all of us. And I think it would be best coming from you."

"I suppose, after all these years of looking and then finally getting something, it's a temptation that's hard to resist. But I thought he catalogued all those things the last time. I know he got paid something by the big boys he brought in. Not that I was expecting much, but I haven't seen a dime. Have you?" he asked.

"He got enough to pay off the boat. But, no. Nothing so far. He said there were expenses and he'd explain. Mother says he's a man of his word." Madison wanted to trust him, and it didn't take much convincing to ease off her questions of the old crusty friend of her mother's.

"This appears to be a new find, and I don't think he's obligated to share it with anyone except you and me."

Madison nodded agreement and then laid her head back on the pillow next to Ned's. She thought about what it would feel like to be rich. She wondered, would it change them? Would he become a different person? Would she? Would it bring more danger than it was worth in the long run?

She decided now was a good time to begin some of her questions. Lacing her fingers through his hair, she asked, "How much time do you have here, Ned? How long do I have you for?"

He hesitated before answering then cleared his throat and began. "I've been giving it a lot of thought. And I want to talk to you about that too. But if Noonan's right, then maybe living here would be my destiny. I've asked for two months' leave. That should give us enough time to sort all this out. After that, I'll have to make a decision about going back to Coronado."

Her heart was dancing in a cascade of rose petals.

His warm eyes saw all the way to her soul. "I felt when I arrived tonight that I had come home."

"You have."

"What if I don't have to leave?"

"What about the Team, Ned?"

"The Team—all the Teams—will still be there. But maybe I won't."

Madison's breath hitched as if she'd been punched in the stomach. "Don't say that!"

"Look at the chances for happiness we all don't take? None of us knows how long we're going to live, Maddie. I'm not afraid of that. But I do have some control over where I spend my days—however many I have left. And who I get to spend it with."

Her eyes filled with tears, and she let them fall back into her hairline and into the pillow below. He said a lot in those few words, but he had not asked her to marry him. She was hopeful that would be part of the picture, but she didn't want to ask. She wanted to hear it without having to request he say so.

She preferred to dream about what it would be like to wake up every single morning with him at her side. Not just for a few stolen evenings or days or weeks at a time, but *forever*.

She was going to keep her hopes up but still protect her heart. Her mother had always been the one to believe in fairytales, but Madison grounded herself in reality. Now all of a sudden, their roles were reversing.

"Talk to me, Madison. Tell me how that makes you feel." He kissed the side of her face and then pulled back after noticing her tears. "Have I hurt you somehow?"

"Not in the least, my love. It's just all so overwhelming. But I do like having you here, and I wish you never had to leave. So if you're looking for some kind of encouragement about perhaps leaving the Teams, I'll happily be your cheerleader."

"I'd love that, Maddie. Let's see what Noonan has to present to us. I want this to be a decision we make together. I want to make a life with you, Madison. I can't be a Boy Scout forever."

It wasn't the whole enchilada, but it was pretty darned close. She wasn't sure about the new dive being a dominant factor in his decision, because it really was his decision to make whether or not he remained a SEAL. What she wanted to hear was that his love for her was all he needed, and it wasn't there.

Yet.

But yes, it was close. She allowed herself to feel giddy. She knew pressuring him or asking for an outright commitment might not get the result she was hoping for. So she turned and said, "You'll always be a Boy Scout, Ned. You can't help but save the world. It's just that people in Florida need some saving to. And I love the idea of never watching you run off to some dangerous place to save others when there's so much you could do here."

"Sweetheart, something tells me we're in for a big adventure. We better buckle up and get ready for the ride of our lives."

His passionate kiss transported her to a cloud floating in the sunset overlooking the Gulf of Mexico. Maybe her mother was right.

Maybe miracles really do happen.

CHAPTER 4

Sleep deprived, Ned brought Madison to the restaurant they arranged to meet Noonan at. This was the morning of his big reveal, and Ned hoped pulling himself out of a bed he could lazily spend the next twenty-four hours in was worth it.

Normally, he'd be irritated with his two or three hours of sleep, but last night had been the best kind of tug-of-war. It took a couple hours before he could finally relax and really enjoy the bedtime play. That was always one of the highlights of being with her. Her energy drove him forward, bringing out more passion than he'd experienced before. He would've loved her anyway, of course, but this was just icing on the cake.

He wished he didn't have to wait to explore what moving here to Florida would mean for them both. This new dive had altered his plans somewhat. But he'd give Noonan time, especially if it involved some adventure and the possibility of finding a fortune to stake their new life on.

Madison snuggled closer to him, reached over, and grabbed his orange juice, having finished her own first. He pretended to be territorial of the sweet liquid but followed it up with a smile. She could strip him of everything he owned, and he'd still die a happy man.

"Do you know, Ned, I could get used to this? I kind of like that discussion we had last night."

Her big blue eyes looked up at him, and he was hooked all over again, wishing they'd spent an extra hour or two at home in bed before showering and getting down here.

"I'll have to adjust to sharing my O.J."

"Small price to pay, right?" she said, brightly.

"I don't ever want to get *used* to this. I want it to be fresh and exciting and something different every single day."

She gave him back a puzzled expression.

"Oh, excuse me," he quickly added. "I didn't mean a different position every day. That's not what I meant. What I mean is…"

She placed her palm over his lips. "I know what you mean. I feel the same way too."

How did he get so lucky?

She was so easy to love, firm and stubborn in all the right ways, funny as heck when the mood struck her. So damn sexy and logical at the same time. He was reminded of that math teacher in high school who wore big black horn-rimmed glasses but had a knock-out figure, cute little upturned nose, and pert lips. She used to drive him crazy, and at those very moments, when he was at his peak of intoxication and fantasy, she would call on him to answer a question he never heard.

Just then, Noonan La Fontaine darkened the restaurant entrance, searched from side to side, and spotted them in the corner. He was carrying a briefcase, but all the rest of him was pure pirate captain. He didn't dress up. In fact, as he sat down, Ned realized he probably was wearing the same clothes he wore picking him up at the airport the day before.

"So how are you two love birds?" Noonan sat the briefcase on his left in the booth, leaning across the table. The waitress filled his coffee cup without him asking.

When neither of them jumped to give Noonan an answer, he waived his fingers in front of their eyes and remarked, "Oh! I get it now. This won't take too long, so you'll have plenty of time for a nap this afternoon. But first, we eat, and then we talk about some business."

"Is this the same site we were at before? Or have you located something else?" Ned asked, ignoring Noonan's instructions.

"We've harvested almost everything from that site, and of course, we're not allowed to disturb too much of the seafloor for environmental reasons. Now it's up to the archaeologists to do their research. There turned out not to be very much silver after all. Most everything will be placed in the University's Museum collection for future study. Lots of interesting tools, utensils, and such, but not much as far as silver or gold bullion. The Galleon and what was left of the barge are not ours any longer."

Ned was surprised at this, and it must have shown on his face.

"What happened?" Madison asked.

"Lawyers! How I hate them. Contract fine print. The University has a ton of them. And tree-huggers, environmentalists combing over every splinter down there."

"There are no forests down there," said Madison.

"You'd be correct. But there are kelp forests, no trees. Doesn't mean they don't look for them, though. Some group claimed the site was home to an endangered starfish colony, if you can believe such foolishness. How can you endanger a starfish? They grow back arms and legs, and you can grow new starfish from amputated legs just like cactus! These scientists are nuts. Fuck science!"

"Sorry to hear that," Ned whispered. He glanced

around the room to see if he'd stirred up any interest amongst the other patrons and found none. "Keep it down, okay?"

Noonan interrupted him. "You remember Travis and Gary, don't you?"

"Just get to the stuff we can understand, will you?" Ned insisted, lowering his voice and requesting Noonan do the same.

"I had to give up before I used all my proceeds fighting them off. So it's done. I gave them the site. Washed my hands of it."

"Done? As in all done, Noonan?" Ned asked.

"I know you are telling yourself how could I turn over the site? Well, I'm not, really. The part that landed at the bottom with the figurehead? It's not the most important part. It probably was a huge weather event, likely a hurricane that occurred soon after the ship went down, separating the two halves."

Noonan leaned forward and whispered, "I've located the stern. It lies nearly twelve miles from the original crash site, and I think it was towed there originally, perhaps as part of a salvage operation to be re-explored later. Something happened, either natural or man-made. It looks like someone tried to cover parts of the wreck up with rocks and boulders, or somehow an event occurred that rained down these rocks, but over time, the entire hull has been filled with sand."

He gulped his coffee and tapped his fingers on the table, surveying the restaurant one more time before he dug into his briefcase and pulled out a leather pouch. Inside was a cleaned and partially eaten-away mesh of fine chain, with clusters of large stones the size of his fingernails.

The dog collar.

"How the hell…?" Ned started.

"Someone found it maybe more than a hundred years ago. It had been cleaned and dried, partially repaired. See?" He showed where portions of the links were replaced with new material.

"But how did it get preserved so well?" Ned asked, fingering the collar.

"It was buried in a jaw that remained relatively airtight, in a crypt, probably interred with the guy who found it. He didn't fare as well as the collar did, I'm afraid to report."

"How did it get back in the ocean? That's where you found it, right, Noonan?"

"Yes. Old sly Davey Jones went and took it back. This nameless soul's remains were reclaimed to the Bay in the crypt he was buried in, during the great hurricane of 1863."

Noonan pulled out some large photographs, which were grainy at best, and handed them over.

"I had these taken last week before I called you, Ned."

Ned looked over the poor-quality, colorless image.

"This looks deep, at least deeper than the other one," he mumbled.

"And that's exactly why no one has found it. In fact, I even suspect there's been a minor earthquake below, because only portions of this vessel can even be seen. Take a look at this, though." He pointed to a dark pile of rocks, not like piles of cannonballs but angled pieces of rock, almost as if the ocean had found concrete from an abandoned roadway.

Ned pointed to one enormous dark grey structure, the crypt. "I don't see a single thing in this picture that makes me think of anything about a shipwreck. Why do you think this is the hull of a buried ship?"

"Oh! Very astute!" He demonstrated a number of dark gray striations in the bed floor. "These are not only draglines, but I believe they will show evidence of the ship's mast. See how long and perfectly straight they are? If she was bottom or stern-heavy, the mast might have been placed toward the rear, not in the center or towards the bow. I think this ship was made for hauling heavy cargo." Noonan's eyes were wild with excitement. He searched between both Ned's and Madison's faces.

Ned was still confused. "But how is the ship's mast,

made of wood, lasting three hundred years?"

"Because this particular vessel I traced back to the lady. Remember the figurehead that we found, a unique identifier and unlike anything else we'd seen? Remember?"

"How can we forget?" Madison answered.

Noonan continued. "I checked with the University of Florida maritime archives, because I felt like perhaps some academic had done some kind of vessel research and didn't realize that we had one of these here in Florida."

"One of what?" asked Ned.

"This ship did not come from Spain or Portugal or England. This ship was a privateer, a pirate ship. I think it was originally built or remodeled not in one of the great shipyards in England or Spain, but it was a homegrown variety, perhaps built in the Bahamas, Antigua, or the Caribbean. It puzzled me when I saw the lady with..." Noonan demonstrated with his hands how the statue had extremely large breasts.

"I'll admit, that was a bit strange. They were oversized to put it mildly," said Ned.

Madison frowned at him.

"We're talking about an artifact. Who knows why it was made that way, Maddie?" Ned returned.

"And you would be correct!" Noonan barked, clapping his hands in front of him. "There's a whole story about that. In the late 1700s, Captain Falkland, who was the youngest son of a British admiral, left the family suddenly to seek his fame and fortune by asking for a charter from the Spanish crown. He wanted to be a privateer but was turned down by the Spanish court. In doing so, he also became an enemy of his own family and the English."

"Why would he give up a naval career since he was already a successful captain and a nobleman?" asked Ned.

"Yes, I thought the same thing. Then I read historical records at the museum and discovered, during this period, Spain was not willing to risk a row with the English. There had been a very fragile truce negotiated, codified by a public, high society wedding between an extremely rich merchant in Barcelona and the daughter of an English nobleman at court. And something went very wrong."

Ned sat back, watching Noonan's presentation growing to the boiling point. He knew Noonan's style of giving directions was always laced with a story, a really good sea story. He didn't disbelieve his friend. He only wished the old pirate would get to the point quicker.

Ned decided to demonstrate that by checking his watch, which immediately brought the desired reaction from his father's best friend.

"Hear me out, son," Noonan whispered. "I'm about to make you a very rich man. For that, I beg you to give me a little more indulgence."

"Go on."

"You see, as it turns out, this nobleman's daughter was endowed with a very large upper torso, similar to our lady. For all I know, it could be a portrait of her. The privateer was in love with her." Noonan shook his head from side to side. "I'm sure his affection was returned, but it was a double rejection for the young captain, since his love had been tragically betrothed over his objections, setting off a whole chain reaction of other consequences I'll get to later. Both countries were at the brink of war, and merchants on both sides were desperate to keep the peace, which was good for business. That was the reason he would not be granted his charter to go after the plunder he felt was due him in the Bahamas. But that was *not* the reason Captain Falkland wanted the ship."

"The Bahamas? And what was his reason?" Ned asked.

"Because it was his ship. He designed and retrofitted it for his life of piracy. And he was the captain when it was wrecked."

"His love married the merchant's son, and—"

"No, no, that's not what happened. Captain Falkland was going to target ships docking in the Bahamas, the British Virgin Islands, Antigua, and other places. It turned out that he also had several close friends who'd been conscripted in the most brutal manner to serve on British ships guarding important ports for the English in the Caribbean. He planned to return the favor by stealing them back into a life of piracy, since after their abduction, they were dead to the world anyway. He went there looking for manpower."

Madison leaned into Ned, resting her cheek on his shoulder. He drew his arm up and around her and kissed the top of her head.

"When can we get to the love story?" she sighed.

"I'm almost there, Dear," Noonan said, patting her hands on the table. "Although, it's a sad one, sorry to say."

"So tell me how this ship wound up in the bottom of the Gulf of Mexico, off of the Florida coast then, if all his operations took place in the Caribbean."

"Because, my friends, he was running away. Her father was looking for him, after his daughter was found to be with child, and this child is suspected of being the offspring of the young captain-turned-rogue. The rest of the story is that she stowed away to join Captain Falkland, in the Caribbean, and was never heard from again. The legend goes that she died in childbirth, and to erect a monument to her passing, he had the figurehead created and lashed it to the front of his pirate ship."

"Noonan, maybe it's because I just came over after more than two months of difficult action plans, and my brain is probably not working up to speed. But I'm confused. All these threads are making my head hurt," murmured Ned.

Noonan struggled to draw out the drama further, but even the pirate was getting tired.

Their waitress brought them the omelets they had earlier ordered, refills on coffee, and a whole pitcher of fresh squeezed orange juice. Everyone remained quiet.

"I want to hear about the metal mast," said Ned. "To my knowledge, during those days—unless we're talking about something much, much more recent—metal wasn't used. It was considered dangerous. It attracted lightning, and it was too heavy."

"That's where you're wrong, son. Yes, it was not used commonly, but metal masts were used in places that had access to a particular kind of metal."

"What do you mean, Noonan?" Ned asked.

"In the middle 1700s, gold was discovered in Mexico but also in Columbia as well. Other minerals were also found such as copper, tin, and huge deposits of silver. Since gold and silver were so heavy, anyone who might use them to embellish a ship would be adding extra tonnage to the draw. However, just like how we soup up cars today, some privateers created very intricate and complex designs using plating—converting regular cargo ships into first-class works of art. It was thought some privateers earned so much money in the trades all through the 1700s and 1800s, they would occasionally pour themselves sheets of gold or silver and hammer them into place over their masts. When these caught the light of the sun, they almost appeared like a ship approaching that was on fire. It scared everyone in their wake."

"I've never heard that before, but I can just imagine. So you think this hulk was one of those custom hot rod ships?" asked Madison.

"I do, and I have the proof." He tapped on the long striations in the black-and-white photograph. "It took something rather heavy, if it was dragged, to make lines like this. It could even be these are the actual pieces of the ship's mast, creating a sort of small ridge and valley, the characteristics of the gold or silver metal affecting what kind of plant and animal life attached to it."

"Fascinating. And these pictures, these are your proof?" ask Ned.

"They are, and I also have this."

Noonan punched his hand into his briefcase and pulled out a man's sock containing some kind of artifact. He looked behind him and then scanned the room before he laid the object on the table. It sounded like it was dense, probably metal.

He slipped the sock off and revealed a shiny, six-inch-long half-tube of silver.

Ned was shocked.

"It didn't look like this when I picked it up. I got lucky with a basket and dredged the bottom, and this came up with several other pieces of crude red clay pottery, containing iron remnants that, of course, created lots of associated layers of sea etching. I soaked it for two days in a special cocktail, peeled off some of the sea crust and debris, and eventually got down to the silver itself. Once I removed all the detritus, I was able to polish what was left. And you will see the filigree etched inside silver, the shape of the tube, and the fact that the edges are smooth, and contain holes for fixing this piece to another rounded object like a mast pole. I believe this is one of perhaps hundreds of pieces that adorned the ship."

"So what's the catch?" Madison asked.

"The catch?" Noonan barked, irritated. He slipped the object back into his navy-blue sock and tucked it away safely in his briefcase.

"Yes, the catch. You've already found this, and surely, you've laid claim to it. You have lined out people with specialized equipment ready to assist with the dive," she explained. "And just who were your divers and photographers for this?"

"Students. They have no idea we found anything except more artifacts for the University. No idea at all. I had to tow the crypt behind my boat and open it later without prying eyes."

"Oh, boy. We have a couple more Travis characters out there, then," remarked Ned.

"Nope, they've gone. Back home. It was just a Spring Break project, a scuba training project, that's all."

"So you can claim this?" Madison asked.

"It's a technical problem for me, because I was given permission to dive for architectural reasons and happened to find what we thought was a galleon. However, the gold and silver that normally would be carried by a galleon, we could never find. We found some gold and silver and jewelry remnants, but it wasn't really the mother lode we thought we had."

Ned waited for further explanation.

Noonan nodded. "You are due a few thousand dollars, but not the millions I hoped. My partners had to be paid back first, since there wasn't much to salvage. And that was always something that puzzled me and a mistake I didn't want to repeat. The portion of the ship we found didn't have any of this rigging on it, which I thought was logical at first. After all, it's quite common for these wooden timbers to be destroyed, like you pointed out, Ned, damaged by all the storms and currents until they disappear. But when I researched the statue and read the stories about the privateer's silver ship with the mast plated in silver, I knew I had to find the other half of the hull."

"So how did you find it?" asked Madison.

"I calculated the currents and also the records of weather conditions during those years, and I found one hurricane record that we might consider a Category 5 if it were to occur today. It came right across the islands here, long before there were many European inhabitants. There were Native Americans who traveled to the beaches for fishing parties, but I could not find any notation of the storm other than checking old records from the geological survey office. Since they weren't looking for shipwrecks or buried treasure, the record of the Category 5 hurricane hitting an uninhabited island was barely a footnote in history."

"Voila. The hurricane of 1863," Ned whispered.

"Exactly."

"But the damage to the sea bed could be extensive in that size storm," Ned added.

"Of course. And I calculated that the force of the storm would be enough to carry tonnage certain distances, plotting the minimum and the maximum amount they would travel. I also was under the assumption that these heavy pieces of metal would remain together or were somehow connected or lashed and, in this case, obviously screwed to timbers or railings or other parts of the ship instead of being thrown all over the seafloor, and I was right. It remained relatively intact."

"You haven't dived this site?" Ned asked.

"That's correct. And I haven't filed a claim, either. Since this is a deeper dive, I wanted people I could trust to go down and take a look first. Then I'll wade through the legal technicalities of whether or not this find needs to be shared with the family who originally hired me to find the dog collar, which is only a coincidence, or if I could claim the treasure for our own. I'm going to have my maritime attorney look into it. And I want to be fair with them. I'm not looking to cut them out, just want to maintain something for us."

"So this debris field is much deeper than the other site?" asked Madison.

"I believe it's between two hundred and two hundred fifty feet deep. We are going to need special equipment. Ned, I was hoping you could help us out with that."

"I've told you before I can't bring anything the Navy gave me. That's strictly forbidden, but I know some guys who freelance, and I think we can get ourselves hooked up with some prototypes the Navy doesn't have yet. Maybe they'll take their payment in terms of percentage of the find. But that requires us explaining to them what we think we found, which is dangerous."

"And, Ned, I'm going to rely on you and your best judgment to find me characters or partners we can trust. We had trouble with criminal elements the first time, but now this site is way more significant. It might attract a whole new class of criminal element. We're going to have to keep this very quiet."

"Then take my recommendation and stop shooting your mouth off excitedly, Noonan. I've been telling you this since I arrived," Ned reminded him.

He could feel Madison shaking next to him, and he knew she was having some fear issues. He was also concerned about their lack of numbers as far as protection. He didn't like the idea of having to hire too many people onto the dive, since it increased the chances of leaks occurring, which could jeopardize the whole project. But without the additional help, it would be impossible to control the security of this type of operation.

At the same time, Ned was excited about the possibility of finding the rest of the plates of silver covering the mast of the ship. He knew in his bones that it was going to add up to be a substantial fortune—once they located and brought them up.

"What do you say?" Noonan chuckled, scooping up a forkful of omelet he'd allowed to get nearly cold with all his storytelling.

"Well, Noonan, I think you've got yourself one Navy SEAL and a mermaid, if Madison's agreeable."

Madison nodded, her eyebrows raised and her

shoulders rounded. She didn't quite exude the confidence that Ned had, but he could tell she was in.

"And I think I can find you maybe ten guys who might be perfect for this type of caper—men of action, who aren't afraid to protect what's theirs, guys who would be loyal. But the first thing I've got to tell you, Noonan, is this must be a legal dive. We can't get involved in something that is claimed by somebody else or by some foreign entity. You know that happens with shipwrecks."

Noonan sat back in the booth and crossed his arms in front of him. "I swear to you that I will make sure we don't get you guys stuck in something it would cost them their billet. It will be legal, and I'm going to be transparent with you all every step of the way."

Ned wasn't sure if Noonan was telling the truth or just making a hopeful exaggeration, but he still thought it would be safe enough to trust him. For the rest, they'd be looking for good luck. He'd built a career on the Teams based on that one factor alone, since most operations were shitstorms anyway, no matter how much advanced planning was done.

He felt Madison's blood pressure spike up again so asked about it. "Are you sure you're in, Maddie?"

"I can't help myself, Ned. If I don't try, I know I'll regret it the rest of my life."

CHAPTER 5

"WELL, WHAT YOU'RE telling me, Madison, is very exciting. But are you guys sure you're not getting involved in some kind of mess that will get you into trouble?" her mother asked.

"I've known Noonan longer than Ned has, not that I trust him completely. I think you'd say the same, Mother. He certainly has had a lot more experience than all of us combined. He's researched it. He's been doing treasure dives for—what?—thirty or forty years?"

"I think Noonan teased me one time that he could see little baby Noonan's on the beach, digging for shells or using a metal detector to find coins. I thought it was funny at the time, but shortly after that, we had a big falling out. That image still sticks with me to this day." Both women laughed. "He's an odd duck, definitely an acquired taste, but harmless for all the right reasons and trustworthy as far as he knows. His research is good, Maddie, but he sometimes cuts corners."

"But he's honest."

"Yes. He's honest. He tries to be with the facts he has to work with." She frowned and stared out at the ocean. "Just make sure you guys cover all your bases and are extremely careful. Let Ned handle the security. Noonan's just the pilot."

Madison knew that was sage advice.

"Now what did you really come over for, sweetie?" her mother asked, her eyes flashing with mystery and intrigue. Her depth of perception astounded Madison. She could never get away with any secrets, especially involving affairs of the heart. Her mother could pry her deepest thoughts from her just by that look in her eye. And she was a flawless guesser.

"During the dive, we'll be staying on one of the ships for three or four days. We're assembling the team now. Ned is drawing from his ranks in San Diego, from the Teams. I'm reaching out to some of my performance friends who are very experienced at working on dive charters. I hope to God they can cook too!"

Her mother had a belly laugh at that one, clasping her hands together. "You're a good cook, Maddie."

"Mom." She was stern with her answer and wanted to make sure it was clear. "I'm on the dive team period. I don't stay in the kitchen on this one. There's too much to see, and we're going deeper this time." She remembered Ned's admonition. "Remember, this is all confidential."

Amberley stood up, tossing her hair over her shoulder. "Then don't tell me anything more."

Madison rose to take her in her arms. "Mother, you're being ridiculous. You know how careful we must be. I promise to watch my tongue. But nothing. You can't say anything to anyone, understood?"

"I'll manage to keep myself on my best behavior. I promise." Her lower lip mimicked a pout Madison knew she must have given her mother when she was a toddler. "Sounds like you've got your hands full. I can only imagine the entertainment on board. Navy SEALs, your show buddies. That could be a very interesting combination."

"Ned is going to try to pick married guys."

"Oh, sure. That ought to work." Amberley winked at her daughter.

"We need people we can trust. What they do in their off time is their business. As long as we have their loyalty, that's what we're looking for."

"So you need help with Otis, then."

"Well, yes. Would it be possible for me to bring him over here, so he's not left alone in the bungalow all day long, since I don't want you to have to be running back-and-forth between our two houses? I'd just like him to have a safe place to be and be given food and water regularly."

"The street urchin who found a home in your hearts. I think that's very sweet, and of course, I'd be happy to watch him over here. Does he still sleep with you on the bed?"

"Absolutely. And he'll keep you up all night if you don't let him."

Amberley stretched her arms to the ceiling and then bent over to touch the floor with her palms touching her toes. Madison was impressed that her mother was still so limber without doing any formal exercise, except walking. Lately, she hadn't either, and if it wasn't for the heavy lifting she was doing at the Salty Dog, she would be in worse shape than her mother. It kind of tickled her.

"So the man of the hour dropped you off, and when is he coming back?"

Madison looked at her watch. "Soon. Unfortunately, and the timing of this is horrible, my car is making all kinds of noises, so he's taking it over to the mechanic to take a look at it. I'm hoping for the best, but fearing the worst."

"I hate cars. That's why I stick to shopping within golf cart distance. If I need to go somewhere else, I'm going to be either hitchhiking or getting a ride with a friend."

"Tell me you've stopped hitchhiking, Mother."

"All in good time, dear. Soon. How about that?"

"It's dangerous! You read the stories, I'm sure. That's just not smart, Mom."

"Don't lecture me, Maddie. Life is dangerous. Every part of it."

"But—"

"Oh, come on. I much prefer driving my cart. No need to worry." She held her hands at her hips, staring right back. "Really."

"Well, I imagine it saves you a ton of money. No fill-ups."

"Exactly." She added, "Besides, the darn thing is so much fun to drive. Nobody expects this gray-haired woman to be driving a golf cart, often with people falling or hanging over all over it. It gives the young kids, you know, the teenagers, a double take."

Madison resigned herself to failure when it came to arguing further with her mother. She accepted the fact that Amberley refused to be run by fear, and it had always been this way.

There was a long silence between them, as Amberley sat back down on the couch, put her feet up on the cloth ottoman, and leaned back to face the ceiling. "I think there's something you're not telling me, sweetheart." She sat up again, stared into Madison's face, and demanded, "Spill it."

Madison was mortified that her secret had been

discovered. She thought she'd been so good at covering things up, at least lately, but ever since Ned came back, her skills and techniques were rusty. Everything in her life had been thrown off-kilter, not that she was complaining, but just everything was off.

Her mother's intuition was always spot on, and she would feel like an undersized fish that had to be thrown back into the water if she didn't just come out with it. So she took a deep breath, blew it out, and repeated it one more time. Then she began.

"You probably think I'm pretty naïve, but I have a couple of things that are bothering me about Ned and me."

"Only a couple?" Amberly's eyes were wide and questioning.

"He's come out here and asked for time off. The Team isn't deployed right now, of course, but he's asked for two months, and he expressed the opinion that perhaps he won't go back."

"Oh my God!" Her mother's expression was hard to read. "Isn't that good news, Maddie?"

"I-I just can't tell you right now. I can't determine how I feel about it. And I just don't know why."

Amberley took her hand and gently caressed it. "Even a good change can be hard. Adjustments. Maybe you just have to get used to him being around all the time. Or"—she paused—"is that the problem?" Her mom angled her head and studied her face. "So has there been talk about him staying here with you permanently, as in getting married, settling down, raising a family?"

Madison wished she could give her a different answer, but the truth was going to have to work. "It's what I've been telling myself I've wanted ever since he walked into my life. I just don't know, Mom."

Her mother's touch was gentle. "Sweetheart, I can't help you there. It's your life. Your choices. Answer me this. Did he actually say something specifically about marriage or not?"

"Not specifically, and maybe that's what bothers me the most. He knows I love him, and I know he loves me, and he talks about us being together forever, but I keep waiting for, you know, the formal proposal. Am I wrong to not get my heart set on something until I hear that?"

"You would have to ask me that question, wouldn't you? I'm afraid I'm no help to you here. I wish it weren't so."

"I don't understand what you mean, Mother."

"Well, when I was your age, that was the last thing I ever wanted—to be married, tied down, raising a family. But then when you came along, I guess that shifted many things, but it didn't mean that I wanted to get married, settle down, and be a wife. Not with your father. I was certain I wanted to raise you on my own. There was never any question about that."

Madison knew exactly what her mother meant. The only person in the world that her mother would have stayed with her entire life was Ned's father, Jake Silver. However, Madison wasn't going to make her admit it tonight. But she still had a question.

"Mom, is it wrong to want at all? I worry that I'll pressure him too much, that'll make him feel cornered, or we'll stop being fun, and would you just listen to what I said!"

She was even frustrated with herself, pulling at her hair, then scrambling to her feet, and pacing back and forth. "I've told myself hundreds and hundreds of times that I wasn't at all interested in being someone's sometimes wife nor was I interested in being someone's wife at all. I rather thought I'd follow in your footsteps, but I was open to whatever the sea dragged in. I certainly wasn't going to go searching for it."

"You're talking about the ring and the ceremony. Not the falling in love part, right?" her mother drilled her for an answer.

"Exactly. Maybe you did your job too well. You did it. So could I. I'm convinced of it. But I still want the whole Happily Ever After when it is all said and done. Is that wrong?"

"Of course not. You have a right to want anything

at all. But a woman should never chase. She might like to *be* chased, but she should never chase. However, I'm not sure that answers your question. And maybe I don't have a good answer for you, but I wish I did."

"Do you think I should ask him? Should I just hint that I'd like to know if, in his mind, this was going to be the relationship of his life like it is for me?"

Amberley carefully answered her with a whisper. "Only if you can handle the answer. Go ahead. Ask him. But be ready for the truth when he answers you. If you're sure, and I mean one hundred percent sure, you can live with the answer, then satisfy that curiosity, ask him, and see what he says."

"What if he feels pressured, then?"

She shrugged. "That depends how you ask him, my dear. There is a nice way to do this, you know. You show respect for yourself by asking him. Come from that place. Not the needy place, which isn't real, anyway. But only when you're good and ready. Not until then, Maddie."

Her mother released her hand. Madison stared at her lap. Her head was nodding, yes, but she still wasn't sure. "I wish I knew what to do, Mom. I really want this to work."

"Of course you do, sweetheart. It will all work out one way or the other. It is an important direction and decision in your life. Probably the most important one.

Unfortunately, these decisions have to be made without the benefit of years of experience. If I told you what I thought the right answer would be, that's based on years of knowledge. I've fought a lot of wars over this—relationships being lonely or being happy. You will have all this experience one day but don't have now. That's what makes it so unfair."

"Yes. I can see the logic in that."

"But I give you this, and perhaps this non-answer will help. He's a man of action, just like his father was, and he doesn't want to be told what and how to do things. But he does want to be sold on something that he doesn't think he can create all by himself. Men are afraid of things like that when it comes to relationships. That's why so many of them are afraid of women. On top of all that, you have to make him think that it's all his idea."

Her mother's advice hit her chest like a ton of bricks. She was no more sure of what she should do next than she was when she sat down the first time. All she knew was that she loved Ned and wanted to bring joy and laughter into his somber life. She was certain she could do that. But she wasn't going to beg. She wanted to be his choice, someone he couldn't live without, because that's how she felt about him.

"Thanks for giving me something to think about, Mom. I do know a couple of things about myself that just popped into my head. I won't beg, and neither will I wait in line."

Amberley beamed with fresh light from within her soul. "That's my girl!"

The two women hugged.

"Here's one last piece of unsolicited advice. Don't do what I did. Don't let him get away."

Just then, Ned burst through Amberly's front door. "Well, it's official. Your car is dying, and it's about time we bought you a new one. Since we're waiting on Noonan anyhow, I think that's what we should do tomorrow. What do you think?"

"Why, Ned Silver, are you buying Madison a car?" Amberley asked.

"I guess I did say that, didn't I? Well, how about I take it out of my share of the proceeds? A gift in exchange for putting up with me here these next few weeks. What do you think, Madison?"

"We could always borrow Mom's golf cart."

CHAPTER 6

NOONAN CHARTERED ANOTHER dive boat, the Lucky Strike. It was also approximately seventy feet long but had accommodations for four. Between the two vessels, they could sleep up to twenty people, including the old captain himself.

"I only want people you can vouch for. We have a lot of work to do bringing up, charting, and cleaning the artifacts, but we also must be mindful of our security concerns. I want us kept discrete and safe. Your SEAL brothers seem like they'd be the perfect fit."

"I'm gonna have to check with my LPO on whether or not they can spare the number of men you're asking for. If Kyle says I've got to go outside the teams for our crew, then my task is going to be a little more difficult. But I promise you, Noonan, we'll use only good people that I personally vouch for."

Noonan also informed him he asked Madison to find a few divers that she'd worked with before at

SeaWorld. "Two to four would be the perfect number. Not only would we eat better, sometimes women notice things underwater than a man doesn't. Madison knows several ladies who have hired on to help as boat crew on some of these treasure dives in the past."

"She told me, and I completely agree. You won't find a protest here, and neither will some of my guys."

He and Madison were going to spend a few hours in the morning searching for a car, a small SUV of some sort. They were both hoping the dealerships would be interested in taking her old car in trade, fully disclosing its mechanical defects.

But first, he had to make that call to Kyle.

"Geez, Ned. I think I've said it dozens of times, there must be something in the water there on the Gulf coast. You guys get into some crazy schemes, not to mention everybody falling in love all the time. I'm not sure I should ever go there, happily married man that I am."

Ned was pleased he'd found Kyle in a good mood. Their last short deployment had seen lots of upset and friction amongst the members of the team, and Kyle had used every bit of patience he possessed to keep war from breaking out.

Ned had never experienced these issues to such a degree before. He chalked it up to new rules of engagement being imposed upon them by the Navy, their

State Department overseers, and upper management—officers who no longer worked the active ops and perhaps had lost their taste for blood, along with some of their courage.

It was a common complaint amongst Team guys these days. Kyle had confidentially revealed to him that, if Ned wanted a leadership role, it would probably be one of the biggest issues he'd face. He'd have to keep the head shed upstairs satisfied while not allowing them to infect his guys in the unit.

Perhaps Kyle had reached his limit. Maybe his time with the Teams was waning. If so, he'd be sorely missed. The whole platoon looked up to Kyle Lansdowne. It had taken a dozen or more years for him to earn that.

Ned decided to get right to the point, sticking to the script he'd written in his mind. "So how many can I recruit?"

"And you're talking something one hundred percent legal? I mean, no clandestine operations, no unusual fire power, no specialized naval equipment taken in secret?"

"No. That's not it. What we're looking for is boat crew. Smart good guys who can help us with security, experienced divers extremely comfortable researching the shipwreck we're going after. I'm not allowed to say much, but I hear your concern. I can guarantee that everything we're doing will be abiding by the law."

"Ned, I don't know exactly when our next little vacay is, but I think a little Florida R&R probably wouldn't hurt any of the guys. Are you going outside Team 3?"

"I may have to. I was thinking Andy and maybe boatman Wilson Nez, Danny's cousin. And I was going to ask Danny as well. You know I hang with Damon quite a bit, Tucker, TJ, and others. I was even thinking of Zak, if he wanted a little adventure, though he might be too busy with the winery."

"You're going to need certified divers, Ned, so some of the retired guys might not work. Depends."

"Okay. Then I'll give you a list before I make the final selection, and if you got anybody on that list who isn't solid or for some reason you don't want to be invited, I will honor that."

"I appreciate that, son. But it is your gig."

"Out of respect to you, Kyle. That's important."

With that bit of encouragement under his belt, Ned began the long process of creating his roster. Kyle approved it within minutes after the email was sent to him. He began making his phone calls, needing to be cryptic while explaining that it was necessary.

It took him less time than he thought to round up a crew of twelve solid guys, including one of the best dive instructors, Crater Meade, who had his own long list of successful treasure hunts. Pieces of eight and other artifacts littered his office at the dive shop.

Although Meade was technically a civilian instructor, sometimes the BUD/s instructors would add him to the training faculty, especially if a newly reorganized Team was needing extra skills with an eye to training for a mission that was going to be almost entirely water bound.

Madison made her calls as well and was waiting answers. She readied herself for their car shopping adventure.

Ned needed to impart some car shopping advice. "If you see something you really like, Maddie, I want you to look like you don't. The worst thing you can do is to let the salesman know that you're absolutely in love with a particular car."

"I know how it works," she said. He could tell she was slightly annoyed with the process. Ned knew it would be more of a challenge than she thought. In the end, his instruction was useless.

Even with the early warning, they bought the first white VW compact SUV she drove. She even told the salesman, "I think I'm done here. Let's get this one. Okay, Ned?"

And that was that. He was unable to negotiate more than a few hundred dollars for her trade-in, which was a crying shame. He made her promise she wouldn't let any of the other Team Guys she was going to meet know about what they'd bought or how they negotiated.

Maddie also threw in another little surprise. "My mother advanced me some money, so we can pay her back from our plunder. Is that how you say it?"

Ned laughed. "Close enough, sweetheart. As long as you're happy, I'm happy too."

By early afternoon the next day, Ned's whole team had been selected, with only one change. Kyle agreed on all of Ned's choices. Andy Carr from Seal Team 4 would join along with Jason Kealoha, Damon Hamblin, TJ Talbot, and Tucker Hudson, who were all enthusiastic about the possibility of making some extra money. He wasn't sure Jake, Lucas, or Zak would be interested, but in the end, all three agreed. Zak reminded him that it had been a while since he'd done any kind of operation but he had kept his dive certification active and was looking forward to the challenge.

Crater Meade was a little more difficult to convince. He was making big bucks already with civilian dive trainings and recruiting new instructors for his school. He had also planned a surfing trip to Australia and Fiji, which would now have to be postponed.

But in spite of it all, he said yes.

Danny Begay was thrilled with the opportunity to work with his cousin Wilson Nez.

Everyone was scheduled to arrive over the next twenty-four hours. Ned told them their expenses and airfare would be reimbursed at the end of the trip. He also asked them to bring equipment suitable for a two hundred fifty-foot dive, as well as any other specialty equipment, cameras, or electronics that might be useful. Crater was helpful in obtaining some specialized equipment they would need. Those outside Kyle's command were asked to get permission from their respective teams.

Madison found a large Airbnb House close to the beach for the guys. She then rented a house several doors down from her own bungalow for the girls. It would be tight quarters on the Gulf, but there was no reason why they couldn't spread out a little bit and enjoy the beach before the adventure.

All the next day, Ned delivered back and forth several of the members as they arrived. All the girls arrived in one car driving from Orlando, about two hours away.

That evening, the group circled for a bonfire, barbecuing steaks and veggie burgers, and getting acquainted. Ned could already see several illicit hookups in the making, things he was going to have to watch closely.

They got to bed way too late but stayed to do clean up then took a long moonlit walk down the beach. He could tell Madison was nervous. Hell, he was too. But tonight, it was all about enjoying the cool breeze coming off the Gulf, holding hands, and letting the sounds of the ocean rock them both to sleep.

CHAPTER 7

MADISON ESCORTED HER team picks to their new quarters a few houses from her bungalow. Each of the three ladies had their own tiny bedroom, since the house was converted from a modest two-bedroom home to a short-term vacation rental. The market for beach property had soared through the roof, and she felt herself lucky to even find a place so close. She explained this to them when she demonstrated that, unfortunately, they'd all be sharing the same bath.

Georgia Allen was Madison's oldest friend, a Southern girl raised in Florida and South Carolina, with bright red hair and penetrating green eyes. She'd been the performance team's leader when they did five shows a day together at SeaWorld before Madison moved over to the Gulf and gave up her "water dancing" routines for the Salty Dog and the company of her eccentric mother and her quirky friends.

"We'll be in the water so much and then on the dive. I could care less about pampering in a bathroom. And no makeup! What a blessing," she said in her soft Southern accent.

Serena Brooks had been raised in Southern California, where she attended college in the greater L.A. region on a volleyball scholarship. She stood six foot three and had nearly made the U.S. Olympic Volleyball Team a decade ago, before she fell in love with synchronized performance swimming and moved to Florida to work at SeaWorld. An injury took her off the schedule for several weeks, but she continued to train and supplemented her income during her performance seasons by doing charter crewing for dive captains, similar to Madison's experience. Maddie was delighted she was able to join them because she was an excellent cook and was expected to take charge of the galley.

"I'll be all right as long as you don't use up all the hot water. That I gotta have every morning, no matter what."

"We'll make sure, right, ladies?" Madison asked the group.

Liz Fong, from Hawaii, spoke up, "You just heard Georgia doesn't even shower, so we're cool."

"I didn't say that," protested Georgia.

"Well, it sounded like it," Liz insisted. "But just to show I'm still a nice girl, I'll let you go first."

Liz liked to call herself the human cannonball since

she was the shortest of the former group and usually would be tossed in the air while doing tumbling routines. She had only been in Orlando for about four years but was already looking for a change of scenery and more than a little adventure to her life. The idea of crewing with a dozen or so SEALs and former SEALs, plus the prospect of earning a small fortune, was exactly what she'd been looking for.

Even Ned's insistence that all the divers were either married or had someone didn't faze her in the slightest. Liz was also an excellent oriental cook, having grown up working in her parent's family restaurant on Kauai as soon as she could hold a rag. But she let it be known she didn't expect to be stuck solely in the kitchen.

"The house comes with a golf cart, but we can ride together if you meet me at my place," Madison began. "I'm at 701 Gulf. Now, I'll give you a chance to get settled. Noonan wants to have a preliminary meeting in two hours down at the Blue Water Sports Club, about two miles south of here. So come on down to my place no later than an hour from now, okay?"

"What about a car?" asked Georgia. "You got one of those we can borrow? I understand rental rates are outrageous here."

"They are. And often there isn't anything available. Let me work on that, but as of right now, no, no car. Most of what we'll be doing we'll be doing together, anyhow, so I wouldn't worry. Serena, you and I can do the food shopping this afternoon, unless Noonan wants to get involved. Usually, the men handle the alcohol. Since you're the designated cook, we'll have to come up with some menu plans this afternoon."

Serena nodded. "I already worked on a few anticipating that. Also, I have to check out the equipment before we take off too. Just in case I need something. Usually, these boats are pretty bare."

"You'll have that chance today after the meeting. Both the Bones and the Lucky Strike will be there. My guess is we'll be on the Strike, since the galley is twice as large," Madison answered her.

"Works for me," Serena responded. "I brought a few tools of my own."

"Okay, meet me down at my place in about an hour, then. I have to run a short errand but will be back shortly. You all have my number. If you have questions, just text me. There should be an extra set of sheets and towels in each of your closets. Speak up now if you need additional blankets as it can get a little chilly on the shore if we get some wind. Depending on how things go, we might be coming back here two or three times during the contract, but I'm not positive. We've leased the place for three months, which Noonan thinks is more than enough time to get the job done. But I don't know exactly how long you'll actually be living here. I'd take everything with you when we take off tomorrow morning."

Satisfied everyone was set and unloaded, Madison drove back to her place to finish packing. Ned would be meeting her at the Sports Club dock site later with everyone else.

She picked up Otis, placing him and his dry as well as wet food in her new little SUV and headed to her mother's house. Otis was nervous at first, peering out the window with a forlorn look, pacing back and forth on the second seat bench. But just as they turned into her mother's driveway, he began to calm down and slouched over onto his legs folded in front of him. Madison connected his leash, tucked the bowls under her arm while holding the bags of food, and directed Otis to follow her to her mother's front step.

He sat, waiting for her mom to answer the door. Without being asked, he stepped through the doorway.

"Would you look at that? Already feeling at home, I guess," said her mother. She pulled the bags of food from her daughter's arms as Madison disconnected the leash.

Bending over, Madison spoke directly to Otis. "We're going to be gone for a few days, Otis. I want you to be good. This nice lady took very good care of me, and she'll do the same for you too. I have it on good authority she likes to spoil her pets, so you'll have an easy time of it."

The mutt looked up at her adoringly, seated, as if to attention.

Madison padded his head, scratching the hair between his ears. "That's a good boy."

"When do I—?"

"You feed him about the same time you have breakfast and dinner. And then take him outside at least twice before bedtime. I told you he'll sleep on the bed with you, I think."

"I've not had a dog in so long. Hope I don't kick him off the bed," her mother added.

"Happens in our house all the time, especially now that Ned is back. Don't worry about it."

She said goodbye to her mother with a hug and gave Otis another pat, turned, and drove back to her little house to meet up with the ladies. As she got out of the car, she could already hear their music blaring over the narrow alleyway on the beachside of the island.

She thought it was a little early for a dance party.

She might have been in a more festive mood, but she knew a lot more about the risks than they did. There may come a time when she'd have to explain to them that two people had lost their lives on the previous dive. Since they were experienced crew, she didn't think she needed to mention unsavory characters who liked to hang around watering holes looking for information they could sell or use. Or that just the preliminary research Ned and Noonan had done might have put them all at risk, inadvertently.

The three newcomers knocked on her door just as she was zipping up her pack. She greeted them and motioned for them to sit in the living room. "Just gathering some maps and a couple of sketch tablets. I'm almost done. Help yourself to the refrigerator."

She had her back turned as Georgia made her way to the kitchen.

Georgia sighed. "It's water or beer. I'm guessing water?"

"Bingo," whispered Serena.

"I've brought my own water," added Liz.

Georgia handed a bottle of water to Serena. "What about you, Madison?" she asked.

"I'm good. Have a bottle already," she said, holding up her light pink glass water container on a strap.

"They have a desalinated supply on board, or do you know?" asked Serena.

"I know the Bones doesn't have one. Not sure about the Strike, but I'd guess it does. Will you find out and let us know?" Madison answered.

The ladies pulled up to the club, following Madison to the rear by the pier. Several tables had been placed together. Noonan was talking to Ned and several of the men while others sat and awaited the start of the meeting. They stood when the ladies entered the area.

Liz Fong took a seat next to Crater Meade, whom she'd gotten acquainted with the night before at the get-together. Serena and Georgia sat together, close to where Madison was standing. Ned joined her, giving her a kiss on the cheek.

Noonan barked out the meeting orders and then lowered his voice as he read off his notes.

"Most of you don't know all the details of this dive, so I'm going to spell it out and then give you a chance to bail now. Otherwise, I'm handing out consent forms, a notice of non-responsibility, and insurance options. It's important you read over this document carefully so you know your rights and the risks involved.

No one spoke, so Noonan continued.

"I've consulted my maritime attorney, and we are a go on making application for a claim. However, I want to be sure the full coordinates of the project—I don't want to encroach on anyone else's claim, and I want to give us as much room to explore as we can legally get. We're looking for silver. In this case, we are hoping to find a supply of tubes of silver. And we're looking for plates of silver. Not plates you eat from, but plates that would be attached to a mast, to a special railing, something to enhance the beauty of a corsair, a rogue ship sometime before the Civil War, perhaps closer to the Revolutionary War."

He showed the silver tube without letting anyone touch it. He held out several pieces of plate, roughly molded and hammered. Some were decorated in etched filigrees. Others bore rough pour markings or unfinished adornments.

"I want you to explore in teams of three or four. We're going to determine the size of the field and then work off a grid. Everything we find gets catalogued and marked down. I know I don't have to tell you this, since you're all experienced, but no one takes home a trophy. Not until the claim is filed."

T.J. Talbot raised his hand.

"Yessir?"

"You don't have a claim to dive for this? What guarantees do we have we won't get into trouble trespassing on someone else's land or claim?"

"That's a fair question, son," Noonan answered. "I've catalogued a few items, like these here I've shown you today. But the instant I file a claim to bring up silver, the State of Florida will have their hands in everything we do. We need to make sure what we're diving around has not already been claimed, either as a historical treasure or a claim filed but now abandoned for salvage. We'll want to identify the vessel or vessels to determine their origin and their payload. But, if I'm right, these are individual wrecks of vessels avoiding the long arm of the law. Ownership may be hard to verify."

"That would be you have no permission, then," T.J. stated.

"Technically, yes."

"What's our protection, because I was told that would be in place," T.J. insisted. "I made a promise to my LPO and my wife that I wasn't going to do anything illegal, and I'm sticking to that plan."

"I'll see to it that you do. But right now, from my research, I find no claim of this wreck I'm wanting to investigate. In this case, we know the ship was lost at sea somewhere around 1862 or 1863 because it never reached its destination. But no one knows where it went down. The only thing I've determined is that it is at least ten miles, probably more like fifteen, off the Gulf Coast of Florida. Beyond that, we have to establish that we have the rights to keep what we find or at least a significant portion of it. That's the chance I'm offering you. The moment we discover something is illegal about removing anything from the site is the moment we stop. Is that understood, son?"

"Yes, that covers it. So what do you think we have here?"

"I think we have a clever and rogue pirate, once a decorated naval officer, who possibly was a wanted man for crimes he probably didn't commit. He operated under the noses of the French, the British, the

Portuguese, and Spanish. His home base might have been somewhere near the islands of Antigua, Barbados, or Bahamas. In fact, I think this ship was made on one of those islands."

Judging from how quiet the patio went, everyone sat to rapt attention. Madison knew more than many of the other crew members chosen, but even to her, the story Noonan was painting was exciting.

"I think I even know the name of the gentleman, the captain of this ship that went down. You're going to have to make a decision, because after that, there's no turning back. Ask yourself if you want to be part of this or not. Either way, we won't discuss anything about the project until you've read over and signed this document."

Many of the people on the patio had heard tall tales of getting rich from the treasures lying at the bottom of the ocean. They'd just never placed themselves in the center of those stories.

Until today.

CHAPTER 8

NED WAS PREPARING to head home for an early turn-in after preparing maps, coordinates of where they were estimating the site was located, and reading over the rules for recovery of artifacts and treasure. The good news was that it was nearly fifteen miles off the coast, which made permissions more likely if they had a connection to a research institution or school. Noonan had worked with the University of Florida, so they would have to be brought in carefully. Everything had to be by the book legal since the SEALs would be risking their careers if it weren't so. And even though portions of the find would have to be shared with the institution and the State of Florida, there would still be enough to make a small fortune for all of them.

But there was bad news, and Ned knew he was going to have to tell Madison and the others about it soon. He also wanted to hear from the maritime attorney himself before he could proceed, since it was a new wrinkle.

Ned felt like a dumbass for not questioning the towing ashore and opening of the crypt Noonan admitted to doing. He should have known right away that there were Federal laws against tampering with gravesites, human remains, and desecration of historical relics. Noonan should have known about those laws, yet he ignored them. Was Noonan being deceitful or just trying to cut corners in his fever to obtain treasure?

The bottom line for Ned was that it didn't matter whether it was done on purpose or not, Ned couldn't be a party to grave-robbing, and he couldn't get the others involved, either.

Going out to the Gulf of Mexico—regardless of other claims, distance from shore, registration of wrecked vessels—without knowing the consequences of the discovery and opening of a crypt would be aiding and abetting a third-degree felony. Noonan had said not to worry about it, that it was being taken care of. However, Ned was hired to worry about all those things, and he didn't trust an attorney he'd never met before, nor did he completely trust his father's old pal. But his fondness for Noonan had perhaps colored his feelings, and now Ned himself had fallen victim to the treasure-fever Noonan had.

The pirate captain was due to return to their little rented office across the street from the fishing club and the pier any minute now. All this was weighed on him the more he thought about it. He had kicked himself across Gulf Boulevard and back again, slammed against all four walls of the little office in his mind when the old man opened the door, giving him a huge grin.

"There he is. You wrap it up?" Noonan asked him.

"Just about. But I got one huge problem to go over with you, and I discovered lots of things I wasn't aware of as I read over all these salvage laws. My ass, as well as my reputation with my colleagues, is on the line here. I'm a man of my word, and I still intend to keep it."

"What's got you all riled up? Show me."

"There's no 'show me.' It's something you know about full well. You opened someone's grave, Noonan. You desecrated a body. That's against the law."

"Oh, that. My attorney is handling that."

Noonan didn't seem to be phased one bit.

"That's just not good enough, Noonan. I'm going to call a halt to this whole thing if I don't get some answers I can verify."

"Go ahead. You can call him."

"I will. But first, I want you to tell me how you plan on 'taking care' of the issue, because I don't see any solution in front of me."

"Sit down, Ned."

They both took a seat.

"You're right. I shouldn't have opened it. At the time, I didn't know what it was. But I knew it was hollow from the sounds it made when the kids tapped on it. Our detector couldn't pick up anything inside. It was encased in lead, I discovered after I opened it. But it was much too light for a solid piece of concrete or for a safe. And there was lots of debris all around. You saw the pictures, Ned."

"I remember. I agree, nothing could have told you what it was. But you pulled it out of the water without permission, nonetheless. Like you did the masthead, the lady."

"Yes, I did. And the lady is now sitting in the University's Museum for all to see. Quite an attractive and well-received display, I'm told."

The old man's eyes twinkled, and Ned knew exactly what Noonan was implying.

"Give me some answers, man. I gotta have them now, or I'm pulling the plug on this whole thing. I'm going to have to eat crow to men of honor who will never trust me again. They all got leave and traveled her on their own dime. And now I must tell them you violated the law. Worse, I knew it and didn't let them know about this."

"No, that's on me. And for your information, I was going to tell them."

"Goddammit, Noonan. *Telling* them isn't the issue. The issue is we can't be a party to your committing a felony. If we're involved in the coverup, we're just as at fault. We could lose our Tridents over it. That's on *me!* How could you do this to me, to Madison, to all of us, Noonan?"

"Listen. Things wash up on the beach all the time. Hurricanes have wiped out whole cemeteries in the past all over the East Coast, in this state, as well as others. They find shit all the time, floating in the water, washed up on land. Sometimes ships run right through them when things float out to sea and find their way to shipping lanes. Japanese glass fishing globes have washed up in San Francisco Bay after having traveled clear across the Pacific."

"Where is the crypt? Where is Falkland?"

"Martin already took care of it. He reported it, said it had been found by someone who didn't want to come forward, which is certainly true, and he was doing the right thing by allowing the authorities to examine it. You're gonna hear a news report about it sometime soon, coming straight from the Coroner's Office. It's been disposed of and is now safely out of my hands."

"And what if Martin decides to turn you in,

Noonan?"

"He can't. He's my attorney."

"He can't help you break the law, Noonan."

"I didn't knowingly break the law, Ned. Only you and Madison know about the collar. I intend to give it to the family in North Carolina after all this is over with. It has nothing to do with the site, except that the man's grave landed right on top, perhaps protecting that site for over a hundred years as a pure unrelated coincidence."

"I have to hear it from Martin himself."

"Suit yourself. I'll get him on the phone if I can."

"Better tonight than tomorrow. Because tomorrow, we must tell the guys and gals or end this whole caper."

"Don't be so hasty. Talk to Martin first. I'll arrange a meeting with him tomorrow morning in person, as well. He drew up all the disclosures, the releases here. He wouldn't have done that if he knew he was violating the law or helping me to do so. You ask him about that."

"I will."

Ned wasn't feeling any better about this whole situation. In fact, he was feeling much worse. Again, he blamed himself, but now anger toward Noonan was boiling in his stomach. Some of his experiences with his father came flooding back to his memory, compounding the situation. It was like he was being taken advantage of by that dick of a father all over again, just as he was starting to put some of those feelings to bed.

"Martin. I'm sorry to call you so late, but…"

Noonan listened to the attorney. Ned could hear a long-winded interrupt, which sounded suspicious.

"Oh, I completely understand. Can you call me after his game is over? It's very important. I need to talk to you tonight."

Noonan signed off and ended the call. "He's at his son's soccer game, but it's at the end of the second half, and he says he'll call me when he can get some privacy. He's in the bleachers."

"Fair enough," Ned answered. "So we wait."

"Show me what you've done while we're waiting."

Ned brought out the maps. He'd marked the tide timetables and weather conditions for the next week. He'd compiled a folder with all the expenses of the rental diving equipment, the cost of leasing the Lucky Strike, supplies for operating both vessels, additional safety equipment, communication devices and readers, extra lines, tanks, scuba gear, and emergency supplies in case of an injury, the marine biologist report on expected plants and wildlife, including a certification there were no endangered reefs or international sites or toxic cleanup projects in nearly the whole eastern half of the Gulf of Mexico, where oil rigs had caused problems in the past. Much of this was paid for by

Ned's own money, and the amount was adding up quickly.

"We're at over twenty thousand dollars, not including the Strike," Noonan mumbled under his breath. "I can give you some money for Madison's shopping adventure with Serena today. I'm assuming…"

"I gave her my card, but I don't have the receipt yet," Ned interrupted.

"Thanks. You're doing a great job of keeping the costs down for me. I've got savings to cover all this, so you won't have to wait."

"I appreciate that, Noonan. This isn't like me. I can't believe I went full speed without questioning all this stuff. Man, I'm losing it," Ned added, shaking his head. "Your attorney better be honest."

"He is. Maritime law is all he does. Went to law school in Norway, also interned with several large European shipping firms. He knows his stuff and has Merchant Marine companies as some of his clients."

Just then, Noonan's cell phone rang. Before he picked up, he pointed to Ned. "Do not talk about the collar. Anything else you want to ask, go ahead. No mention of the collar."

"Damnit."

"Ned, I gotta have your word."

"Okay. But I better get a straight answer."

Noonan answered the call, thanking Martin for returning it. "My partner here is worried about the crypt and how that was handled. Can you explain it to him, like you did to me? He wants to be reassured nothing about that will come back to bite any of us, even slightly."

Noonan listened and then passed the phone to Ned.

"Martin? This is Ned Silver…"

"You old Jake's son?"

"I am."

"Your dad was right proud of you, son. Said you got all the good parts from your mama, and he was damned grateful for that."

"Thank you, sir." Ned felt far from thankful but was going to give the man a chance.

"I was best man at the coroner's wedding to his third wife about ten years ago, but we go way back to high school. I told him I had an anonymous call from someone who had uncovered a body encased in a box. Not a murder, mind you, but in a burial box. We wanted to turn it in, but the caller didn't want to get involved. I asked if they could do that. He wanted to examine the remains, see if there was some sort of foul play first, but he called me yesterday and told me they had closed the investigation and the man, at least they are assuming it was a man from the bone structure, would be re-buried since they didn't have the resources to find his family that far back. He said DNA samples could not be obtained, so that was that."

"I want to make sure none of that taint comes back on me or on the guys and gals we've hired to help Noonan with his exploration."

"No, you're good. I got a coroner's report emailed to me this morning, and I guess I could let you see it. I can't give you a copy. Son, this sort of thing happens all the time. At least it wasn't a murder, because that would have been another story completely."

"I'd like to see that report, if you don't mind. This whole thing has got me spooked. Sort of a bad luck omen, if you know what I mean?"

"Noonan did the right thing by telling me about it. The coroner said the box was consistent with the way burials were done above ground over a hundred fifty years ago in this county. It probably was lost years ago and just took a while to resurface. We've got records of cemeteries pulled to the sea all over Florida. Not a damned thing we can do."

"Should I come to your office in the morning then? About what time?"

"I'm coming in at eight. Meet me after my secretary arrives at eight-thirty, if you can. I'll put the coffee on."

CHAPTER 9

MADISON MISSED OTIS already, so called her mother to make sure the mutt wasn't misbehaving.

"Are you kidding? He's wonderful, Maddie. I gave him some instructions on how to paint a floral landscape, not that it will do him much good, but he did manage to get some acrylic in his whiskers. He didn't like the taste much."

That cheered Madison up. "I expect great things from Otis," she said. "Can't wait to see what he paints in the sand next time we take him for a walk."

"You might not get him back. I'm growing rather fond of him already. He might just decide to stay here. But you could always visit. I promise you that."

She heard Ned's truck pull into the driveway and signed off. "I know I don't have to say it, but take lots of pictures. I'll be missing him something terrible when we're out on the Gulf."

"Will do. You're leaving in the morning?"

"We are. Supposed to, anyway. There are so many last-minute details, and we're on a race against time due to some weather concerns. Also, we've got this big crew here who are anxious to get started."

"Well, be safe. Best of luck. If you can, send pictures yourself."

"And I probably won't do that," Madison said as she watched Ned come through the door. "Now I really need to go. Ned's home."

She could see right away something wasn't right with Ned.

"Uh-oh. I know that look. You're scaring me," she sighed.

Ned gave her a quick hug and then stood facing the ocean, which was smooth as glass in the early evening moonlight.

"Do we need to take a walk on the beach?" she tried.

"No," he said to the glass door. Then he abruptly turned. "But I'm worried about a couple of things." He stared into her eyes. "The biggest problem I have is that I have to keep something from the team guys. I don't like having to do that."

"Keep what? We have no secrets."

"The collar. We can't mention the collar or where it came from. I'm trying to figure out a way that I can let them know about what Noonan found, as in the box, but not tell them about the collar. They should know, Maddie."

"I trust your gut instincts, Ned. Do whatever you think is right," she answered. With her hands around his waist, she rocked with him in tandem, trying to release the tension he was rigidly holding all over his body. "It can't be that bad to let them know, unless…"

"Noonan doesn't want me to. He thinks it complicates things, and it will. We might lose the entire crew."

"Why?"

"Because it's a felony to disturb a grave or human remains. I discovered that when I was going over some of the protocol for the survey and exploration. We could go to prison for disturbing that man's grave."

"The grave that the hurricane unearthed, you mean?" Madison stood with her hands on her hips. "It's not like he went to a cemetery and started digging someone up. That didn't happen. It was Mother Nature."

Ned angled his chin, shaking his head. "I didn't see a footnote stating that if a diver didn't know it was a grave and disturbed it, then it was okay. No such rule about that, Maddie. I don't want any of my guys to get in trouble for my fuck up."

"But you didn't know that—and Noonan had no clue what was in that box—unless he really did. In that case, he's been lying to us." Madison frowned and released her arms from his hips. "Are you saying you don't trust Noonan now? He's hiding something? Where is the coffin, anyhow?"

"It's a crypt, or was. It's been turned over to the coroner's office. The remains are going to be buried in an unmarked grave. After over a century, with the water seepage, DNA testing wasn't possible."

"Did you help Noonan actually do that? Did you see the remains?" she asked.

"Hell no, Maddie. I wouldn't touch that for anything. But I'm kicking myself all over the place that I didn't think to ask more questions before we had the guys come out here. That's my fault. And I feel I should own up to it."

"Then you should. Better that they decide they don't want to get involved than to risk them finding out afterwards that you knew something and didn't reveal it to them in time to make a different decision. You would expect the same from them, right?"

"I would. And I promised Kyle and all the guys that everything was above board. I just didn't think about the issue of the dead body. I feel stupid about that. I let them down."

"No, Ned. That's your good and honest nature kicking you in the gut. You've got to act on that. I don't think you have a choice." This was one of the reasons she loved him so.

He nodded. "You're right, of course. But I'm checking with the attorney in the morning first, and then I'll talk to everyone and make sure there are no second thoughts. But the hardest thing is going to be not having the story spread to too many other places or the news could get hold of it, and then our dive would no longer be a secret."

"Maybe it was folly to think we could keep it under wraps, Ned," Madison whispered. She was hoping he took it as a suggestion, a comment, and not a criticism. She felt how on edge he was.

"I must make this right, honey. I just won't be able to live with myself otherwise. It will be my job to convince both the attorney and Noonan that this information has to be revealed. If not, then it falls to me to curtail the whole mission. I'm just going to have to admit that I made a mistake and now I'm trying to fix it."

She didn't envy his task, but she was certain it was the right thing to do.

THE GROUP GATHERED at the SEAL house, or so it had been nicknamed, sharing takeout from one of the great pizza kitchens on the island. Ned and Madison were the first to leave, and they told everyone to plan to have their gear ready by noon. Ned apologized at the late start but indicated there were some additional details he had to take care of first.

As they drove back to Madison's, she knew that the group would take advantage of the fact that they didn't have to get up at dawn, which is what they had planned, so some partying was in order. Ned told her that not everyone would be in favor of that and would elect to call home instead, but he wanted them well rested when he had the little talk.

She agreed with his approach and told him so.

"I have no doubts you'll do the right thing. You'll figure it out, now that we know," she said.

She requested to accompany Ned and Noonan's meeting at Mr. Zinski's office, and he agreed. She called the ladies, letting them know she'd be available by phone in case they needed her. And she offered to lend her keys to Serena in case she needed anything they'd neglected to pick up earlier. The gesture was greatly appreciated, and they agreed on a spot she could leave behind her keys.

They showered and turned in early, but the sleep was fitful, both of them tossing and waking each other up several times.

Madison knew part of her feeling uncomfortable was the fact that Otis wasn't there with them on the bed. She'd forgotten what a comfort he'd been when Ned was away. Now she missed him even more.

Just before they fell asleep, Ned got a text from Noonan stating he was not going to be able to attend the meeting but would catch up with him afterwards.

"Figures," Ned whispered. "Just my fucking luck." Madison pretended to be already asleep.

IT WAS A gorgeous Friday morning in Clearwater, where Martin Zinski's office was located. The lobby had a sweeping view of the Gulf, the huge beach and community below, and the little boats out on the water streaking across the blue expanse like tiny comets in an early evening sky.

Ned could see immediately that Zinski was indeed a heavyweight in maritime law and commented so. His business was booming, and they both were impressed by the organization. The office bustled with several junior associates and clerks brightly doing worthwhile work they obviously loved.

They were shown to the conference room around the corner, which had a two-sided version of the large window from the lobby.

"Geez. I can't even remember my name; this is so impressive. All my meeting notes just flew out of my head," Ned muttered.

"I agree. It's stunning," she answered.

Martin Zinski's handshake was tight, and Madison noticed Ned wince slightly, trying to mask his surprise.

She could see this also caught him off guard. On top of that, the attorney was probably no more than about five foot five inches. He was fit and trim, graying at his temples. He didn't resemble anyone old Jake, Ned's dad, would have ever known or Noonan either for that matter. This realization was almost as distracting as the setting.

"Thank you for coming in. I'm really slammed. Where's Noonan?" Zinski barked.

Ned rubbed his palm with his other hand. "He texted me and said he couldn't make it. I'm guessing he wants to let you do all the talking."

"That's just like the man. But never mind. I'm hoping I can assuage your fears without him."

Ned was waiting to be convinced. As Zinski opened up a thick file, Ned added, "I'm a man of my word. I should have asked about the legal issues of Noonan hauling this crypt back to the pier. Should have been the first thing that came to my mind, but it wasn't. Now I've got twelve men and three women ready to help us with the project, and I'm inclined to pull the plug on the whole operation. I can't ruin my career in the Navy—I'm a fuckin' SEAL—sorry…"

"No, no. I understand," Zinski blurted. "Let me…"

"These Team guys would never let me step into something without assurances I gave them first. Turns out, I didn't know everything I should have. I even gave my own LPO a guarantee of sorts that everything was going to be done by the book—proper and legal. He released these guys, or acted to help get them released, so it's on him too. I can't have everyone going off without some 'out-of-this-world-type' exceptional piece of information changing my mind about this mission being scrapped, Mr. Zinski."

"I get it." He turned to Madison, nodding. "Sorry I didn't introduce myself to you. That was rude. Pleasure to meet you. You are Amberley's daughter, right?"

This also surprised her. "Yes. Boy, you're well informed," Maddie said with a smile.

Zinski shook his head. "Not really. Small town. That helps a lot."

He directed his attention back to his file folder and produced a piece of paper with the letterhead of the Pinellas County office of the coroner.

"This," he said, tapping the document, "should be all you need to see. He says right in there that an unknown, unrelated person accidentally found this grave and wanted to do the right thing by turning it over to the authorities and enlisted my help. They examined the contents, which were nearly destroyed except for several of the long bones, which had partially turned to stone and were crusted with what we call sea concrete—deposits of organisms we find everywhere here. Cause of death was indeterminate, no apparent evidence of foul play, and it was consistent with other types of crypts that have washed up on our lovely shores for decades. The remains were logged, catalogued without any active DNA, photographed, and will be buried again within the next few days. That, my friend, is the end of this long story."

"But what if the facts turn out to be otherwise?" Ned asked.

"Is this a crypt? Do you believe this is a crypt?" He showed the pictures of the broken concrete and lead liner from the burial vault.

"Appears to be."

"Are there remains there?"

Ned examined closer, and there did appear to be one long thigh bone with some smaller ones, all laying parallel to each other, none of them with marks or striations on them, and not broken, altered, or sawed. "I think so."

"We have no I.D. We have no DNA. What we really have is a biohazard that has to be disposed of. We have no cause to believe the man was carrying something contagious, do we?"

Ned shook his head. "No."

"So we dispose of the biohazard quickly after cataloguing it and keep the public safe. It was the responsible thing to do since there doesn't appear to have been any kind of crime or foul play."

"But it's against the law to tamper with dead bodies."

"Are you saying Noonan chose to tamper with it?" Zinski looked hard into Ned's eyes. "It's an important question, Ned."

"I don't know how he could. There's barely anything there."

"Right again. Now we could make up all kinds of theories, but on the basis of what? We have no other evidence pointing us to the direction other than an accidental find. Noonan did the right thing by reporting it. In this case, he doesn't have to reveal his name, and I'll make sure that never happens, as well. He doesn't want or need the notoriety. As his attorney, since it isn't required, I'm going to honor that."

Zinski blinked several times but didn't take his eyes off Ned.

"I want to tell the others about the body." It was out of his mouth so fast she was sure he hadn't thought to choose his words carefully.

Zinski shrugged. "Fine by me. I'm not asking you or any of them to lie about it. It's just that there's no need to reveal it until after you've done your dive, because it has nothing to do with it. But if you go around talking about it, well, all bets are off. You might as well all go home. So no, I don't mind that you tell the team. Make sure they understand they undermine the whole operation in the way that story gets told. It's not illegal to stumble upon a dead body. It's illegal to try to cover it up without alerting authorities. There's a huge difference between the two."

CHAPTER 10

NED WAS NERVOUS, and he knew he wasn't exuding confidence like he should have been. He noted Madison was discretely watching him, as if noticing a crack in his armor and waiting for something to fall apart. That irritated him no end. It was why he had always preferred the lonely, uncomplicated life of a single SEAL, since he didn't have to explain his actions to anyone else—anyone else who would care about him, that is. His mother had been like a shadow those past few years as his father wasted away and prepared to leave this world.

He'd seen the upsets and marriages crumble while men in his platoon were deployed in godless countries, witnessing unspeakable horrors. Or when they were trying to overcome ridiculous odds: their small Team against bands of roving hired mercenaries, cutthroats, and villains who would even make Stalin look like a cat sitter instead of the butcher he was. In the middle of all that shit, they'd have an argument with their wife about the kids or the car payment or how they didn't feel loved and why couldn't they call more often. There were good Team wives, and there were those who never should have signed up for this duty. Guys who should have known the pressures would be too much for certain women. He'd seen guys shot trying to cool down an argument in the middle of a firefight.

They'd laugh about it afterwards, but it left scars, all of it. Ned considered himself lucky never to have gotten snagged. He'd always figured he would be a good husband and father when he had time to garden, work on his truck, or put new sod in the backyard—the easy stuff of life. Not this stuff.

But all that was before Madison, and now she was a factor, someone he opened up to. By doing so, he brought her along too. So whatever happened on this dive, it was not only going to affect the men he felt he could die for and his leaders—the good, the bad and the ugly—but it would affect Madison.

He told himself he'd had years of practice controlling his nerves, thinking clearly, and strategizing to accomplish missions. Kyle had noticed it and recommended him for OCS. So he must have been doing something right.

Most days, he just did the best he could.

With the stakes so high, he felt the pressure. *"Pres-*

sure makes the weak shatter and the strong become stronger. No other way it works," his LPO had said more than once to the Team before an op. Kyle was a good example for him. He went out every time. He chose the guys who would do certain dangerous jobs, knowing there'd be a good change they'd get injured or worse, and he had to do it anyway. Or when something went wrong and he had to order someone to put their life on the line, do something he shouldn't have to ever be tasked to do, and lead him to that opportunity to prove they all were heroes. He had to get everyone home, safe, as intact as they could be.

The dangerous injuries were the scars no one could see, just like that pretty lady on the plane described. The good doctors understood the fighting man and his unique needs. They were constantly testing themselves, looking for that weak link. Close to breaking, they had to pull it off like a hero. If it came to that, Ned had always hoped that he would die with dignity, a hero, show some of the younger guys how to do that just like he trained them to dress a near-mortal wound before evacuation or how to carry their equipment so they didn't stumble over something and kill themselves by accident. They all taught each other everything.

These men and women he was going to speak with in a few minutes were looking for him to do the same today. It didn't matter that the air was warm, the water was crystalline and bright blue, or that billions in gold and silver still slept in the grip of the beautiful Gulf of Mexico just waiting for the right person to come along and claim it all. The dangers were all around, whether it be the sea life, pirates, or just plain criminal elements. Florida didn't look like some inner city with graffiti tatted and tagged everywhere.

It looked like paradise, but it was still dangerous as hell.

Wilson and Danny, the two Navajo boys from Arizona, came up to him for a private conversation. The group was assembling at the office, which had been a last-minute change Noonan made in case things got hot and they needed secrecy.

Ned had never noticed that, although the two were first cousins, they looked like twins.

Wilson spoke first.

"Hey, man, I really appreciate you including me in this op. It's one hell of an adventure. Danny will tell you I've worked really hard on my diving and took any class I could to stay up on my certification, even though, if I did my job well, I'd be the one in the boat picking up all the rest of you frogs. You never know, so I kept it going so I could compete if I had to rescue someone."

"I've heard about you. You're our motor man too. I kinda like having someone to second Noonan's opinions on the equipment on these boats. You see something that is about to fail or doesn't look right, you let me know, understood?" Ned answered.

"Oh, roger that. And if you want me to tweak anything, well, I won't tweak anything I'm afraid of breaking. I'm not that kind of mechanic."

"Nah, that wouldn't do. Fifteen miles is too far, especially with our equipment, to have to swim back to shore. And we may have to anchor the dive boats and take the dinghies. I understand you can soup them up something special, Wilson."

"Yes, I can. I sure can." Wilson, who was nearly a foot shorter than Ned, stood like he was two feet taller instead. He held out his hand for a shake, and Ned pushed it aside.

"Thank me when we get back to land safely and the mission is accomplished. Otherwise, I might be the one you blame for getting you into a clusterfuck."

Danny had a belly laugh over that one. With his arm around his cousin, he said, "He can get us out of Dodge so fast they won't even know we were there."

Ned loved having them on the Team because of their grateful attitude. They never took their opportunities for granted and worked everything the hard way.

He surveyed the group, and as Madison and her girls entered the cramped office, greeting Noonan with hugs that made him cringe, everyone was accounted for.

"Okay, listen up, everyone."

Noonan hung back in the corner, his arms across his chest, a grey shadow crossing his forehead down across his nose and chin.

"First, I'm going to need to collect your consent and bio forms, and we'll get to your questions in a minute. Mother Nature gave us a little time, and now there isn't any rain in the forecast for the next seven days. That's a good omen as they say."

The group mumbled a general agreement.

"But I got something serious I have to discuss with you, and I'm not going to lie. Some of you are going to be pissed."

The grumbling immediately stopped. The only sounds in the room were traffic noises from outside.

Half the room was still waking up. Several men had deep creases in their forehead at the prospect of having to listen to something they'd wished they didn't have to. Most everyone else had clenched their jaw, bracing for the final instructions, the last-minute changes. The SEALs were used to this. The ladies, Ned surmised, not so much.

"It's come up that we had a little issue a few days ago. I'm going to apologize to all of you. I was not made aware of it until yesterday, or I would have mentioned it sooner. But I need to tell you about it, and I need to make sure you are still in on this operation. Everyone has to be solid, understood?"

Most everyone nodded silently.

Tucker Hudson, the biggest man there, affectionately nicknamed "Shrek" by most the wives and girlfriends of Team Guys, as well as his own wife, had to take issue with it right off the bat.

"Goddammit, Ned. Just fuckin' get to the point. I could care less how you feel about it. Give me the crap and let me make the decision. Stop treating us like we're teenagers afraid of cutting ourselves shaving."

T.J. and Jake Green laughed. T.J. punched him in the arm.

The women bore shocked expressions, and not from the foul language, either. Even Maddie looked scared.

"Okay, here it is," Ned began. He gave a wink to Madison before he continued. "Noonan here discovered a crypt that had been washed out to sea sometime in the last hundred plus years—probably remaining there since about 1863 or so. We have record of a hurricane that came through these parts before there were many European settlers. The Native American population inhabited these parts for centuries before. I discovered that this crypt did contain remains of someone we can't identify. Noonan hauled it out of the Gulf before he knew what it was, and that's what created the problem."

"That's it?" T.J. barked. "That's the shit?"

"Hear me out, T.J. It's a federal crime to tamper with human remains. Noonan did the right thing, the responsible thing. Through his attorney, he reported the find, and the attorney arranged for the crypt to be turned into the coroner's office here. After careful review, they've cleared any issue they might have had about the body, foul play, as this sort of thing has happened over the years—actually, over decades."

"What do you mean 'cleared'?" Liz asked, using her fingers as quote signs.

"The body was anonymously surrendered to the coroner. Under the circumstances, Noonan didn't have to give his name, and we want it to remain that way. Our concern is that it might interfere with the dive, not that the two are related. Do some of you understand now?"

"So what's there to decide?" Jason asked. "They're not looking for Noonan, right? He's not a fugitive, isn't that correct?"

"That's right. It's case closed. But you might hear of it on the news. We want all of you to make sure and not contribute to the conversation or the accuracy of any reporting that might come up. But the most important thing is, I wanted to tell you because if any of you are uncomfortable now and want to back off, I will understand. You can leave."

"But what does this have to do with the dive in the first place?" asked Andy Carr.

"It was on the sea floor, right on top of what we believe to be the remnants of the wreck. We don't think it had anything to do with the wreck. It just happened to land there, but we really don't know."

"So Noonan's cleared of any wrongdoing, right?" Damon asked.

"Yes, that's right."

Ned looked at the two Navajo boys, who were extremely closed mouthed and showed no emotion. He knew a little about their culture, because he'd read about the invasions in the South Pacific and how it affected the Navajo Code Talkers who had to navigate through floating bodies during that bloody campaign. Many of the men had to go through purging ceremonies or were sent special herbs by their families at home to ward off the evil spirits they believed came from the dead. He didn't want to call them out to embarrass them, but he knew it was something they would be thinking about.

"If any of you would prefer not to dive the site because of this, no problem." Ned didn't make eye contact with Danny or Wilson.

"Are we sure there aren't any more graves, Ned?" asked Georgia.

Ned shrugged. He hadn't thought about that. "To be honest, I can't say. But we don't see anything from the pictures we've reviewed that looks like what's already been removed. We wouldn't be asking you to go down there otherwise."

There was a pause while everyone worked on their private thoughts. Ned added, "Of course, if we find anything that appears to be human remains, we have to stop, catalog it, and report it. We are not allowed to remove anything without that protocol. But first, we comb the site grid by grid, make a final determination how much area we're talking about, and search the perimeters to make sure we've looked at everything. We document everything because artifacts and historical objects have to be recorded, so that when they are turned over—in this case, to the University of Florida—they have a reference point to the conditions of where they were found. A map, if you will, of how they lived on the ocean floor."

Tucker uncrossed his arms and swore. "Fuck it. I've seen dead bodies before. I've even caused some of them myself. As long as I'm not going to be hauled away for touching this stuff, makes no difference to me whether it's a crypt or an oil drum. But I sure as hell am going to look ten times closer. That's a fact."

Several others stated their agreement. T.J. said he just wanted to get out there in the water and stop wasting time. He palmed his disclosure sheet into Ned's chest. "Here, this is my answer," T.J. said, turned, and walked to a far wall.

One by one, everyone, even Danny and Wilson turned in their slips, without a single defection.

CHAPTER 11

MADISON RODE ALONG with the other ladies and several of the Team Guys on the Lucky Strike, piloted by Wilson Nez. The ship was much faster than the Bones, and at regular intervals, Wilson led them on a circular tour of some of the tiny islands that dotted the Gulf, being careful to avoid the shallow parts. The entire west coast of Florida was bordered by a shelf, containing some very shallow areas. The average depth was some six hundred plus feet, but the site they were working on was a mere two hundred fifty or so.

The beauty of the water mating with the horizon was highlighted by the gentle sun and a touch of clouds, which tended to keep everything on the cooler side. It was ideal diving conditions. And if the weather held, it would also make for some ideal starry nights and calm waters—always a welcome occurrence since they would need their sleep.

Danny, Wilson's cousin, was fascinated with the

variety of sea life, including dolphins, who liked to run alongside and race with the ship, and sea turtles, looking like dark green ink spots on the otherwise clear turquoise water.

Sport fishing was allowed in these waters for selected species, but no one but Noonan had an active permit. Jason Kealoha had indicated they could be catching their own food and having fish fry every night, but everyone knew it was important not to get caught doing anything without proper permission. It would be explored the next time they came back to port. If the weather held, they'd be done with the mapping and preliminary photography work in three days' time. That was the goal. Then they could seek out their permissions and return to do the actual recovers and exploration.

Everyone had their attention focused on two things: the appearance of other boats in their vicinity and what particular areas they wanted to come back to that drew more interest than others.

Ned was co-piloting with Noonan in the Barry Bones. Madison noticed that one of the motors was smoking slightly and made a mental not to let Noonan know about it.

Noonan slowed down, searching his sonar for the coordinates he'd logged. The Lucky Strike followed behind at a good distance, giving the Bones room to slow down quickly if they needed to or double back and re-approach a particular area.

The ocean floor showed up littered with debris from oil drums to solid evidence of other small craft or sport fishing vessels ruined by some of the strong hurricanes frequenting this area. But there were dozens of dark areas that were quite large, which indicated a literal vessel graveyard. She was surprised they didn't see any other vessels with the naked eye. Damon and Jason took turns scanning the horizon with their small binoculars, very new tech and highly specialized with add-ons, and which could also go IR at night, all courtesy of Uncle Sam. It was just some of the equipment most of the SEALs had as standard issue. Four of the men brought their re-breathing units as well, just in case.

Danny and Wilson also brought along Wilson's drone, a piece he was working on and hoping to one day sell to the military. It had a twenty-mile range and could send a signal to their computer on board, which could print out color copies with a tiny printer no bigger than an iPad.

Madison was fascinated with the device when Wilson showed it at the get-together two days ago.

He also told her that the tiny device on the drone would even calculate the wind speed and the temperature. It had a memory so that, as it traveled, it began to make an all-weather map, even locating some possible underwater elevations, although that was still being perfected.

She was amazed how inventive he was.

Both teams were issued coms they used on missions, their Invisios, so they could talk back and forth without tagging a cell site. There had been a lot of major smack talk going on all during the trip, although she couldn't hear a word of it. Based on the looks she got, the laughing and basic chatter she knew that she was being targeted in some of their comments. But she also knew none of the ladies would escape the fun play and mock ridicule that was just part of their community and came out at every bonfire or family party. Her friends had thick enough skin to handle it.

Serena was whipping up something in the galley for dinner that smelled like a seafood stew and cornbread. She and Georgia were having a catch up on their love lives while Liz had her nose in a romance book. Zak was trying to help but got delegated to cutting up onions, tomatoes, and celery. She could hear him describe their winery and all the catering they'd done for weddings and special events over the ten years they'd been in business.

"How'd you lose your eye, Zak?" Georgia asked.

"On a mission. Cape Verde, off the coast of Africa. We were protecting the U.S. Ambassador. I got shot. A fragment lodged in there and took my eye. But I still got one left. I requalified expert on everything I used to shoot before, but they still rolled me out on a medical. We got a little settlement, so heck, we bought a piece of land, an old winery site."

"I might be looking for a job," Serena said, "After all this is over. Or maybe I'll have enough money to buy a little place—where did you say that was?"

"Healdsburg, California. Dry Creek," said Zak.

"I could run a little Airbnb and cook for those nice folks coming to visit from my old stomping grounds."

"Very popular, if you can find a place reasonable enough. Amy and I work our buns off. But now the kids are older and able to carry some of the load. They don't get their allowance unless they finish their chores."

"See, that's a good thing right there. You're doing right by those kids by making them work. Can't give them everything they want. That's not healthy. I mean, I grew up in the gym. My older brother had basketball dreams. Everything was basketball. My dad had been a good college player at a small school, but my brother, he had the real talent. They left me alone. I learned to walk on a shiny basketball court. The first time I ran across a game, I not only got trampled but came home with a black eye too. Boy, the kids on the street really gave me a hard time about that."

"Did your brother play later on?"

"No, sir, Mr. Zak. A stray bullet stopped his basketball dreams. Stopped everything for him and for the whole family. That's when I threw myself into volleyball, and I never looked back or thought about anything else until I was out of college."

"Sorry to hear that, Serena. That must have been tough."

"It was. But you know what they say. It makes you tough. All of us kids got a big dose of reality from that. No more sugar plum fairies and princesses. We had to work our way out of the neighborhood by playing ball. And since I could jump but couldn't shoot worth a darn, I spiked and blocked the hell out of that ball and broke a few noses along the way."

Georgia giggled as she scooped Zak's chopped mixture into a bowl. "I'll bet you liked to pancake those pretty blonde girls, didn't you, Serena?"

"Oh, you're bad, my red-haired sista. But it has a ring of truth to it, come to think of it."

Everyone laughed. Madison was glad they didn't know she had overheard them. She had a case of terminal blondeness.

Suddenly, Damon and Jason pointed toward the stern of the ship, where Madison could only see a flat line horizon. But the two men had spotted something. Damon used his earpiece to notify the crew on the

Bones. Madison waited with bated breath.

"What is it?" she asked Jason.

"We got someone following us, I think. They were popping up and down from the horizon, trying to escape detection, but when Noonan slowed down, they didn't react in time and blew it. I saw it briefly before I lost the line of sight."

Wilson appeared next to them. "Can I see?" he asked, holding out his hand for the scope. He yelled at Danny, who had temporarily taken the helm. "Slow down, Danny. Let me see if I can see this thing."

"There it is," pointed Damon. "It's a big one. About this size, maybe bigger. And fast too. Look at the wake."

Madison knew Ned and Noonan wouldn't be happy. "What did they say?"

Wilson was running down the half flight of stairs to the bunk rooms, past the galley, returning with the black case he carried the drone in. Over his shoulder, he whispered, "Ned said to get the bird up there, but don't make it obvious."

Madison watched as Wilson adjusted the wing into the slots in the body of the drone, heard the familiar click and the flipped the locator switch. He got out a small laptop, which he'd told Madison was dedicated to the drone so they had enough battery and storage for good pictures. The green screen went from static to focusing on the floor and his running shoes. Then he excused himself past Madison and asked Danny to slow so he could launch. He sent it due north so it would travel perpendicular to the suspicious vessel. He quickly adjusted his screen until he got a clear picture and then increased the climb to an elevation the ship wouldn't be able to see with their bare eyes.

Placing it on magnification, he got a shot of the ship, which had also slowed down. On deck were four men, and luckily, no one had power scopes, so there was a chance they didn't see the drone launch. He shot several pictures, getting a photo of the vessel I.D. and the name and registry.

"Fuckin Bahamian," muttered Jason. "She's powerful, all right, but I think we could outrun her."

"We could. The Bones would never make it. Go let them know. I'm sending Ned the link to the shots right now."

Danny was twisting around to try to see what had shown up on the screen. "You really think he's tailing us? He looks like he's veering off east of us now."

"Son of a gun," said Damon while using his binoculars. "I think he knows we saw him. He's doing a decoy run."

"Uh-oh," yelled Wilson. "I see three more vessels. We got a fucking flotilla out there, about a mile behind, east of them."

All of a sudden, the warm sunny day became dark and dangerous. Madison knew this wasn't good news at all. Their secret search wasn't secret any longer.

CHAPTER 12

This wasn't supposed to happen, Ned thought. They were nearly ten miles off shore, and thank goodness they hadn't yet reached the site. They had been zigzagging, not traveling in a straight line, to disguise their final destination in case someone flew overhead or, as in this case, a faster ship overcame them.

Noonan was sweating profusely, both because of the sun and the danger that had suddenly popped up.

"I'm heading north, Ned. You tell me if they stay semi-engaged."

"Jason said they were rolling the horizon, trying to stay out of sight. Noonan, I think we got ourselves some trouble."

"Shit. Yes, I agree. But no uniforms, right? It's not a fuckin' gunboat, right?"

Ned chuckled in spite of his own concern. "No, Noonan. Just calm down and take it casual. Breathe.

Heading north is a good thing. We'll slowly maintain toward land in case we have to go for it."

"The Bones isn't made for this," mumbled Noonan.

"She'll be fine."

When word came that there were three other boats behind the one that had been shadowing them, Noonan barked for a beer.

Ned gave him an ice water instead and earned a nasty look. He shouted down to the galley where Jake and Lucas were making sandwiches for everyone. "Jake, I need a cold wet towel."

Noonan was sitting now, wiping his forehead as the sweat poured down him profusely. He wasn't in the sun, as the Bones had a fairly generous upper deck canopy, and with the breeze, it wasn't unpleasant, but it was obvious to everyone he was struggling a bit. Ned hoped it wasn't anything medical, but just like his dad, Noonan wasn't known for taking very good care of himself.

Jake brought the towel up from below. "What's cooking? We got a tail, I hear?"

"I'm afraid so," said Ned as he wrapped the towel across Noonan's shoulders, stuffing it around his neck and into the collar of his flamingo shirt. Noonan leapt to his feet and, with a jerking motion, ripped the towel off him with his right arm while his left hand gripped the wheel. He tossed the cotton towel into the spray alongside the boat.

"Dammit. I don't need to turn into an ice cube. Get me a fuckin' beer."

Ned couldn't recall Noonan ever being so angry, but he was sorry to see this change in demeanor, which was suddenly now a medical symptom, not a feature of his personality. Unfortunately, it reminded him of his dad, because Noonan wouldn't take any advice, wouldn't allow anyone to help him, and screamed at anyone who didn't do what he requested.

Now Ned could see there was indeed a medical component. The vein in Noonan's neck on the left side was stressing, protruding as if it was going to burst open and spray all of them. Ned grabbed his right hand and took his pulse.

"T.J.! Get your ass up here!" he shouted to the other Team 3 medic.

Breathless, T.J. arrived shirtless, still holding a fan of playing cards to his chest so Tucker wouldn't see his hand. Ned grabbed the cards, beginning to ignite T.J.'s anger, until he took a good look at Noonan.

"Noonan, I'm taking you below decks. We can do it hard or easy. Or I could toss you overboard and let the guys behind us pick you up. Your choice."

The big medic didn't give their captain any time at all to think. He hoisted him up, held him backward in a body slam position, and dragged him, kicking and trying to get purchase with his hands at anything he could grab onto.

"Get your fuckin' hands off me!"

"Not having that. You want me to make you pass out? I can do it very easily." As the old captain's legs and arms continued to fight against T.J., Jake grabbed his ankles, holding them so tight that Noonan began to howl. They dragged him down the stairs and into his stateroom, the largest compartment on the boat. Jake sat on the old man's chest to keep him flat on his back. Ned could barely see Noonan's face, but it was obvious his lips were turning blue.

T.J. opened his medic kit, bypassed the blood pressure cuff and went straight for the adrenaline, administered it quickly and then applied the cuff. The results were staggeringly quick. His face lost the ashen, gray look, and his lips began to turn deep red. Tucker brought another cool towel, this time not dripping wet, and dabbed Noonan's forehead, face, and neck.

Noonan's eyes began to water as they darted from side to side. What Ned saw in those eyes wasn't pain or suffering from the effects of a heart attack he'd just had or they'd just avoided. It was shame. He was afraid to show his fear of dying, being taken out by his own lifestyle. Ned was sure of that.

He'd seen that on his dad's face too.

Ned turned his back on Noonan and the men taking care of him, confident that the worst had passed. He buzzed Danny Begay on his com.

"Where the hell you guys headed, Ned? I'm having a hard time keeping up with your pattern. And you've got something going on with one of your engines. Smoking like my Grandma Emma Two Toes."

Ned appreciated the comedy. He loved that about the Teams. When things were the most desperate, they'd see something and burst out laughing so hard they forgot they were too close to death to not laugh in Dr. Death's face.

"Noonan's had a heart attack, I think. He's down in his cabin. T.J. and Jake are working on him. Tucker too."

"Oh, shit. Let me get Wilson to take over then. Is he going to be okay?"

"For now. I'm going to recommend we get him to the hospital, so that means we're taking the quickest way back. You guys stay here, and I'll catch up with you tomorrow, if I can."

"Nope. Not doing that, Ned. We're following you just in case you have an engine failure and need a ride. You probably haven't seen the footage yet. Should have come through on your phone."

"Been kinda busy."

"I get it. Wilson's drone did everything but look up their social security records and blood type," answered

Danny.

"I'm going to call D.C. and make a report, see if we can identify that craft and the owners. Tell me what you saw. Are they military? Any uniforms? Noonan was most afraid of that bunch."

"I'm guessing no. If they'd wanted to highjack the boat, they'd have done it before we got so far out to sea. And besides, who would want that bucket of bolts? How's he feeling?"

"Sheepish. Angry at the world. Embarrassed too. We definitely need to find out whose crosshairs we got in front of. It was not a coincidence, Danny."

Ned made a sweeping arch, having made some good ground in the few minutes they'd been turning back. He swung behind a small cluster of islands, or perhaps one large island with just the peaks sticking out of the water. The water was dangerously shallow there. The larger boat the bad guys had would need to be careful not to get snagged on something as it had a bigger draw. The Lucky Strike was like a fast-moving tank and would plow through anything and had even less displacement than the Bones. It was newer and made of more lightweight material. And that added to her speed.

Danny buzzed again in Ned's ear. "I got an idea. Mind if I place a call to the tribal council? We got some guys with better-than-top-level access to some criminal databases, on a much smaller scale than your FBI contacts. I may not be the best swimmer, since most of us were never taught as kids on the res, but my contacts might be able to help find these idiots faster than your team in D.C."

"Sure, go ahead." Ned didn't want to be disrespectful, but he just couldn't help himself. "So, Danny, I got a question for you. How the hell did you get your Trident? And how did you manage to get invited on my dive team?"

"Oh, my bad."

Ned began to laugh. "No, seriously. How'd you do it?"

"One of my BUD/S instructors was Dine. He took me to the complex one night during pool comp and wouldn't let me leave until I passed. Trust me, I wanted to kill him with my bare hands when it was all over. I don't know by how much, but I passed. I was near drowned, but I passed."

Then out of the corner of Ned's eye he saw the big dangerous-looking behemoth swerve away in the opposite direction, speed up, and then disappear over the horizon in mere seconds.

Danny squawked in Ned's ear again. "See? There's another reason I'm on this team," Danny persisted.

"I'm going to regret this. I just know it."

"That was no boat. That goddamned thing was a

spaceship. We got those on the res too. You know that, right?"

"Good one. Okay, we're gonna head back slower, so I don't blow up Noonan's rig. I'll call ahead for medical to be waiting for us at the pier."

"Roger that. Wilson's put the drone back to bed so I can help the ladies down in the galley. We'll have dinner ready by the time we hit Treasure Island."

T.J. climbed up from quarters and reported to Ned that Noonan was sleeping and his blood pressure was approaching normal range.

"Can you call Bay Care and have someone meet us at the Sports Club?"

"Will do. Bay Care?"

"They have a hospital just over the causeway with a first-class emergency and cardiac unit. That's where I want him to go. We'll settle up who stays behind and watches the gear later. First, I have to make sure Noonan gets treatment."

"Roger that."

T.J. scanned the horizon for the other vessels and shook his head. "All clear for now."

"Thanks, T.J. You getting hungry?"

"I'm always hungry. I understand Serena and Georgia have cooked us a nice meal."

"I've been told the same." After a short pause, Ned shook his head again, laughing.

"I fail to see the humor, Ned. Wanna let me in?"

"I think we'll call this Operation Dinner Cruise."

"Now that's funny."

But T.J. didn't laugh.

WHEN THEY ARRIVED, Noonan was met by the Bay Care Paramedics team and whisked off to emergency. T.J. offered to go with him so Ned could stay behind with Madison.

She fell into his arms, still shaking, but Ned made no mistake. He needed her now more than the other way around. And that was funny how that worked, he thought.

"Is Noonan going to be okay?" she asked.

"I think so. He needs to take better care of himself, but I think, like any good alley cat, he still has a few more lives left."

"I'll get my mother to go visit him after the dust settles. Will he be long in the hospital?"

"Depends on what they find. I'm guessing they'll keep him a day or two at the most, unless something else is going on or he needs surgery. But that might be what has to happen, Maddie. Your mom could be a big help with that, if it should come to it."

"You know she'll do anything to boost his spirits."

Several minutes later, the crew gathered on the Lucky Strike, trying to relax, but also trying not to attract more attention than was necessary. They'd already drawn a crowd with Noonan being transported to the hospital.

Zak brought some of his wine from California, which paired nicely with the Cajun fish dish Serena had made. Ned knew Noonan wouldn't have tolerated the heat levels, but the Team loved it. Ginger brought out a whole pound of Amish butter to slather over their steaming hot cornbread that melted in their mouths.

Then they had strawberry shortcake with huge fresh Plant strawberries, only in season for a few weeks out of the year.

The whole meal was simple but certainly hit the spot. As night fell and the stars came out, Wilson brought out his guitar and sang some cowboy songs he'd learned at the mission school, taught to him by a Jesuit priest.

Ned noted how well their team had bonded already, made up from a diverse collection of members from different cultures, living and working in various parts of the country. It was voluntary, but everyone agreed to stay on board until the next morning when new plans would be discussed.

Jason Kealoha expressed his desire to perform his Haka traditional Maori dance ritual. Before he could begin, just the act of stomping his legs, readying his huge frame for the movements caused the Strike to wobble from side to side. It took several men to stop the dance from ever starting.

It was just not the way anyone wanted to end the evening.

Ned and Madison planned to turn in early as several of their group talked into the night. Guards were posted on regular shifts. T.J. returned with news Noonan would be prepped for surgery tomorrow to correct a heart blockage.

"I'm glad we were there. If he'd have been way out there by himself, I don't think he'd have made it back," T.J. said.

"Is he still talking about the dive?" asked Tucker.

Ned already knew the answer. He was leading Madison down the stairs to their tiny cabin.

"Non-stop," said T.J.

Madison paused. "He's in his element, surrounded by people who have to attend to him. They're a captive audience, and he has lots and lots of stories!" she added.

Ned didn't want to spend any time thinking about what their plan B was. All that could wait until tomorrow. It was an exciting day. One could even say a perfect day. He knew just the way to bookend it.

And yes, the two of them would rock the boat big time.

CHAPTER 13

NED WAS AWAKENED for his shift, which began at 0600. They had spent the night in Ned's cabin on the Barry Bones.

Madison got up with him, bringing her lightweight blanket and pillow. Together, they sat on the bridge, watching the sunrise.

"As many times as I've watched the sun come up on the Gulf, I never tire of it. The sunsets either," she said. It seemed like such a natural and beautiful way to begin a day. She never wanted to be without it. They got to witness miracles every day.

"We're in the tropics. Very unpredictable," Ned answered, agreeing with her. "I totally get why people come for a vacation and stay their whole lives. Like there's some kind of magic here, just as Kyle said."

"Everything is so unpredictable, but it's beautiful in that it's always fresh and surprising here. The warm air, like this morning, just swirls around me and makes me feel safe and whole."

"Or the illusion of," reminded Ned.

"But I feel like I can still relax. And I know there's always danger lurking. But the land, the water, and the clouds—it's like they conspire to take my mind places it's never been before. That's what I mean by different and surprising. You certainly don't want me to worry more, do you, Ned?"

"Nope. That's my job."

That brought silence between them as the full force of the sun hit their faces and then the gentle ocean breeze cooled them off.

In the next berth over, Danny and Wilson were drinking coffee and whispering from the bridge of the Lucky Strike. Wilson waved, and she returned his greeting.

Several club workers arrived early and didn't take much interest. There was very little traffic on Gulf Boulevard, and the water was calm. It was as if all the excitement of the day before, with Noonan's heart attack and the chase involving the unknown parties, was washed away since no evidence of them lingered in the early morning light fog.

Ned's cell rang. He adjusted his arms around Madison's waist, readjusted the blanket, and put it to his ear. It was a call from 202 area code. D.C.

"Ned Silver speaking."

Madison could hear the caller's voice.

"You asked for support in identifying ownership of a certain Martin Starliner, and we've located the records," the young woman on the other end of the line said.

"That's great. Let me—"

"First, this vessel was reported stolen four months ago in the Bahamas. It's owned by a British couple who still maintain the open claim. There is a reward for the successful return of the craft."

"So the people who came after us are not the owners?"

"Came after you? Are you sure?"

"Looked like it to me, ma'am."

"For the moment, let's assume not. Our records show that it remains missing. Your pictures are the first concrete evidence the vessel hasn't been destroyed or parted off and sold to pirates for use in their drug trade in Africa and the Mediterranean. You say you saw this boat last night in Florida? A place called Treasure Island? That's kind of a strange coincidence."

"We get that a lot here. Big vacation resort area. People from all over the world. On the Gulf."

"How did you come across it? You saw it with your own eyes?"

"We did. We were about ten plus miles out, and we noticed them pop up on the horizon behind us. It was part of a flotilla of three other boats that were too far away to get any identifiers. I think they were chasing us. This triggered a medical emergency with one of our older passengers, our captain, and we had to head back to shore. Right now, we're tethered privately at the Blue Water Sports Club, while we await the treatment of our dive captain. Next door and only a short walk away is the Treasure Island Marina."

"And where did the craft, the *Jilly Jean* go?"

"They kept going deeper into the Gulf."

"Could it be that's where they were headed, not following you?"

"Could be."

Madison could tell Ned didn't want to give her more detail.

"Okay, I'll initiate the report. I can reach you on this number if I need further information on something, then? You would be the contact person?"

"Yes, ma'am."

"How many in your party, and what was the purpose of your outing?"

Ned was quick on the reflex answer. "We're a group of old friends just messing around, reliving our college days. Boats, blue water, fishing, and swimming—things we all like to do and never get enough time to satisfy."

He was very clever, and Madison smiled at him,

giving him encouragement for his performance.

It seemed to work.

"I'm going to relay this to the insurance representative and the Coast Guard. We'll reach out to the consulate in the Bahamas to locate the owners. You make sure to contact us again if you see this craft a second time. I'll text you the owners' contact information, as there is a reward posted."

"That's interesting. How much?"

"It depends on the condition of the vessel, but this is a two-million-dollar speed-yacht, a custom special hybrid craft. We'll leave all that up to the adjuster. The information will be in a text message directly to your device."

"Is that it? Aren't you going to send someone to interview us?" Ned asked.

"We have your contact file, Mr. Silver. We'll be in touch. Thank you for the information."

"Let me ask this question, then. Am I to assume that the people who have possession of this vessel are involved in some sort of illegal trade or activity, like drugs or high seas piracy?"

"Most definitely, yes."

"Can you give us any information on suspects or at least what kind of illegal activity they have engaged in, other than stealing the boat?"

"Perhaps the adjustor will have that information.

Often these fast boats are used as transport for human smuggling and drug running, since they can outrun anything with the exception of the Coast Guard cutters. We find them abandoned all over the world now."

"I feel they were directly trying to target me and my crew, personally. Are we in any danger?"

"You maintain contact with us. Please let us know if you see the vessel again, but I'd stay away from them. Do not approach. I'd consider them dangerous, so I'd do everything you can to avoid them. Especially if they're running a group of them together. We understand that, in your line of work, your naval history, this might seem like something difficult to do. But, for your own good and for the health and safety of your friends, I'd refrain from trying to engage them. I don't want to offend you, but we don't need any acts of heroism with this bunch. We need you to stay as far away as possible, and let us investigate and do our jobs here."

"Once again, ma'am, we have no intention of trying to contact them, but can we have some indication of who these people are? Some names? Nationalities? Surely you have something on them, with this kind of theft."

"We're working on it. We'll be in touch, Mr. Silver. Try to enjoy the rest of your vacation."

Madison heard the phone disconnect before Ned

could sign off.

"Don't you find that strange?" he asked her.

"You sure you called the right department?"

"It was our liaison number, the number we're supposed to call when we've witnessed a domestic crime. Shit. Maybe that call was a mistake. I better get hold of Zinski."

In the middle of their breakfast, the Team got word that Noonan had survived the surgery, which had taken less than the five hours originally set aside. He would be staying in the hospital an additional two to three days, and he wasn't allowed visitors until the attending physician was sure the risk of infection was significantly lessened and his heart was beating normally.

One by one, members of the team asked Madison in private what Ned had revealed was the future of the mission, now that Noonan was temporarily out of the picture. They all knew that perhaps he'd never be able to re-join the party.

Madison told the truth. She wished she knew, as well. She knew it was weighing on Ned tremendously and that any efforts she might make to talk things over would only add to the pressure he was feeling. She knew he was working on it. He'd made two calls to the attorney's office before they ate and hadn't been able to reach him.

Meanwhile, costs were adding up. This was not Ned's op. He wanted to be able to release everyone quickly if they had no path forward, at least for now, and he'd told her so. But he was still playing a wait and see game, and he didn't want to disrupt a mission that might still have a prayer of going forward. It just wasn't his call.

T.J. and Tucker had gone to the hospital on Ned's direction, to make sure Noonan had some protection while he lay immobilized, in and out of consciousness.

The crew began cleanup of the galley, routine maintenance of the vessel, and checking the dive equipment, which was a constant job on any of these chartered adventures. Every day started out at ground zero so that nothing got missed or taken for granted.

Wilson found a local diesel mechanic to take a look over the dual motors, trying to assess if it was reliable to take out or not. The SWCC guy hovered over the mechanic so close, asking questions, that the two almost got into a fight.

Just after noon, Ned finally got the call he was expecting. He took it in private, pacing up and down the pier out of anyone's earshot.

Madison double and triple crossed her fingers.

CHAPTER 14

ZINSKI WAS ALREADY aware of Noonan's condition.

"This leaves you in a pickle, Ned."

"You think? I get the strange feeling—call it my sixth sense—that something is about to go down. Something big. I'm just not sure where we stand. Should I send everyone home, wait until Noonan is fully recovered, or go ahead in his absence?"

"If he were conscious, would he give you the power to go forward?"

"I think so. Problem is, I've not done this as often as he has. He had a buddy last year who was murdered. But Gary knew all the ins and outs and had been on hundreds of dives."

"Related to this?"

"No. Those were low life, petty criminals one of our crew met through a drug buy. This time, Noonan didn't vet anyone but me and Madison. And he trusted me to get the right crew. But do I have the authority?"

"Off the top of my head, I'd say yes. If you reasonably think he'd want the project to go on, people on the outside would deem that a smart and rational decision for the betterment of all. There's a university that's going to benefit as well, you know. So that's part of the picture—your philanthropic hero button, as it were."

"I'd rather have a little dose of certainty, please. I've got patches and pins galore, thank you very much."

Zinski chuckled. "I'll bet you do." He sighed while Ned waited for his recommendation. Ned wanted to get the green light. They could figure out how to do the dive, and Madison would be a great help, but he really wanted Zinski's blessing first. Without it, Ned was going to send everyone home and risk the ire of Noonan when he recovered and found out what he'd done.

"Your call, sir. But I really need your advice." Ned purposely laid it on thick.

"I'd say go for it. But I also wouldn't string it out more than a handful of days, maybe three or four max. Keep a captain's log of every detail, every event just in case something goes sideways, and you'll have a record to fall back on. Wouldn't hurt to stress in your notes that you're trying to carry on what Noonan had asked you to do before his heart attack."

"We don't have our University of Florida liaison set up yet, and I don't know who he used there. Do you?"

"I can't assume it's the same person or department. They switch out all the time. Just intending to include them when—and specifically say you expect this to happen—Noonan recovers, you'll turn over what you must and catalog the rest. Noonan had a family in North Carolina who originally tasked him with his first dive. He seemed to be very loyal to them, so you could mention that. Let's play it that you are just going to do the best you can and Noonan will fix everything later on. Does that make sense?"

"Sure it does. But what happens if he doesn't recover?"

"At best we have a problem. At worst, we have a huge problem, maybe even a lawsuit."

"And what about those guys sniffing around?"

"You definitely follow the orders the lady at the FBI gave you, Ned. You stay out of their way and report the sighting of the vehicle. Let the feds pick them up. That's a huge crime they committed. Kinda dumb, if you ask me."

"Sounds like we should get going right away. Get in and out before anyone knows we've been there."

"I think that's best. And don't let anyone keep anything. You've got to control that. You are tight with everyone, right?"

"Madison is friends with the ladies. I've spilled blood with all the other guys or had friends who did.

All except one guy, Crater Meade, who owns a local dive shop. He's a certified instructor and even trains SEALs for the Navy. I don't know him, but Noonan chose him, and he's giving us a big discount on some of the equipment. I think he's okay."

"I don't know why that name is familiar to me, but it doesn't send up any red flags. I may have met him a time or two. So, Ned, are you ready and are you sure about what you're going to do?"

Ned didn't want to lie to the man, but in this case, it was necessary.

"Martin, I think Noonan would be delighted to know we're moving forward. One thing you can do for us is get someone posted outside Noonan's room as a precaution. I have two former teammates there now standing guard. But I need them on the boat with their equipment, not standing in some hallway eating hospital food."

"I have a husband-and-wife team who are excellent. Which hospital?"

Ned gave him the room number and all the other details. They promised to stay in touch, each of them promising to let the other know if there was a new development.

Ned thanked him and signed off. He took several minutes, tactical breathing, working to lower his pulse rate, as he watched the calm waters of the bay and the puffy salmon-colored clouds growing like mushrooms from the horizon.

Noonan, you get better. Not time to show up at old Jake's doorstep. You're needed down here. You'll have time for all your hellos and partying later. This is not that time. Give me a hand. Help me decide how to do this. I need you. I really do.

Just saying those words in his mind gave him more courage. He placed the phone in his pocket, turned, and approached the Bones with an extra spring in his step.

Madison was the first worried face he encountered. "Pack up and get ready. We're off as soon as we can. Now go tell everyone. Help me out, okay?"

She beamed. "Absolutely! You got everything straightened out?"

"Nearly. To acceptable risk levels anyway. Did you work Noonan's grid pattern for your past dives?"

"Only about two dozen times. I even know where he stores his paperwork and maps from past dives. He's got logs and a map closet in his cabin. I can show you."

He grabbed her and placed a big kiss on her cheek. "That's all I wanted to hear, sweetheart. I'm going to need you to take the lead on much of that. I'm calling for T.J. and Tucker to return to the boat ASAP. I'd like to get out of here within the hour. Can we do that?"

"We most definitely can. Both boats are clean, the equipment checked. Wilson even got Noonan's engines serviced, so we're good to go."

"Excellent. You spread the word while I call in the boys."

Their fuel was topped off and fresh water onboarded. Serena purchased some items from the head chef at the Sports Club to replace what they'd used. In one hour and thirty, they were heading out to the belly of the Gulf of Mexico, looking to lift up her skirts and recover her secrets. As the barrier islands disappeared from view, Ned was suddenly hopeful. The dread he was carrying had lifted. He wished his father's old friend well.

He knew he was going to make both men proud. One was clear across the country in California, sleeping off a hard and probably disappointing life. The other one was in the shop being repaired. With any luck, Ned felt he had a shot at redemption for both of them.

CHAPTER 15

MADISON SPREAD OUT Noonan's logs and maps over his old lumpy bed, showing Ned how they had organized the grid pattern from start to finish. He had marked with a pencil sketch where he thought the wreck and debris field was located. Long lines extended south from the bulk of the site. The location of the crypt was noted with the explanation "Concrete Box of unknown origin." Ned had suggested they continue to use that term so no one slipped up later.

"See, these lines are where he said the drag occurred," Madison explained. "Some event moved the hull, we hope loaded down with precious cargo, until it buried itself again in the sea bed. I think he would make sure a double team would follow those lines to where they entered the floor, perhaps excavate down to see if we could find any of those encrusted timbers or the mast. We'd also be looking for semi-circular casings, but the shape isn't as important as how it tests on the metal detector. If it tests for a precious metal, then we work that site in more detail."

"You want me to make the assignments? Do we start with pairs at the corners?" he asked.

"No, we start here, at the end of the drag marks, and go outward, north, south, east and west, until we've made a square, further delineating a grid pattern until there is no evidence of the debris field left and it just reverts to virgin sea bed."

Ned nodded.

"You can make the assignments, though. Pick this center section for the most experienced divers. I think Crater and I could partner that. You could take the upper quadrants with your swim buddy, and so forth. Pair people together who would work in tandem. One takes notes and pictures. The other one excavates and explores, and they trade off in twenty-minute shifts so no one gets bored and misses anything."

"Fantastic. I think I'm beginning to see how it's done. When everyone brings back their drawings and photos, we get a look at the whole field, right?"

"Yes, that's where the pattern is discovered. And hence the theory of what caused the wreck or identifying the ship itself. And it could be more than one. We saw that before on the barge dive, remember?"

On a separate map, Madison drew the proposed grid, starting with deep "skid" marks. Ned labeled the teams for each area, leaving Madison and Crater for the middle section. They presented it to the others after they'd found Noonan's coordinates, dropped anchors, and gathered everyone in the spacious Lucky Strike main deck lounge.

The coms and other equipment were tested and re-tested by each buddy in the teams. Wilson would stay on the bridge of the Strike, while Danny would man the Bones. Liz partnered with Jake Green, but the other two ladies remained in the galley to prepare lunch and to prep for dinner to follow several hours later.

The dive lines and monitoring equipment were only connected to the Strike. The Bones had taken on more as a supply vehicle, except for the storage of maps and items Noonan had in his cabin. But all the more sophisticated equipment and sensors were housed on the Strike.

Madison and Crater descended down into the deep first, followed by the other pairs. Lucas was to remain up top on the Strike to help keep a lookout for approaching vessels and to help Wilson and Danny monitor traffic. If anything was needed, he would be the errand boy for now.

Crater and Madison roved side by side with Crater holding the metal detector until they found the deep grooves Noonan had photographed. In one of them was a piece of silver plate, distinguishable by the screaming of the detector. Madison tried to pry it from the sea bed, with no luck. Crater handed her the machine and used a specialized part hatchet, part crowbar custom tool to get leverage on the object and broke a piece of it off. The shiny edge of the fragment was revealed, and there was no doubt that it was silver.

Madison dropped it into the basket attached with a belt to her hip. She then motioned for the others to pace off four big steps and work in all four directions. Soon, the chatter from the coms was lighting up the enthusiasm as more and more items were called out and identified. They found coils of metal, glass jars, tools, hardware, and some broken earthenware pottery. Ned reminded them they were under strict orders to leave everything on the floor except for the remnants of silver plate they might need to plead their case for further exploration. It was going to be hard to sell Noonan's theory of golden or silver-plated masts, so a photograph was deemed not adequate.

T.J. and Ned found the remnants of a rounded door handle, covered in a thick white crust. They also photographed and studied what appeared to be a pile of lumber that had at one time been lashed together with rope, now reduced to several long strings. As Ned tried to place one in his basket, it turned to putty and eventually disappeared completely.

The twenty minutes went by fast. Teams switched

roles and worked until the edges of the site could be determined. Each group photographed the four corners of their grid using plastic L-shaped markers Madison had given them.

After nearly an hour, they heard Wilson's voice over the com.

"And I have a sighting of a dark blue or black yacht—looks to be a hundred foot or more. It's crossing our path. He doesn't appear to want to come over. And now, he's waving."

"Make sure you get pictures, Wilson," demanded Ned. "See if you can get their call letters on the side."

"I can't read them. I'd get the drone, but he's too close."

"What's he doing?" asked Tucker.

"Stopping, dammit."

"Keep your distance," Ned barked.

"We're sitting ducks," Danny added.

Lucas broke into the conversation. "Hey, guys. I think they mean to board us. He's talking to someone on a radio or sat phone."

"Wilson?" Ned called out. "Get that fucking drone out now. I want a recording of this from overhead. Send a copy to your own devices just in case."

"Roger that, Ned."

"Lucas, give our friends at the Coast Guard a call, let the ladies know what's going on, and then help

Wilson out at the bridge. Danny, you okay? If you have to run a decoy, you do it. There's a Luger and some extra rounds in the captain's locker under the wheel, but you'll have to break the lock to get at it. You do that if you feel you need to."

"I'm on it, Ned. If I have to ditch, do I have permission?"

Madison's heart sank with that last comment from Ned. Was he actually asking him to make a run for it armed with only a handgun? His boat could easily be overcome, putting Danny in grave danger.

"Use your best judgment. But you'll have to explain it to Noonan."

"Ned, we're not staying down here, are we?" asked Crater. "If we got potential bad guys up top, we shouldn't be left so vulnerable. We gotta get back on board."

"I'm one step ahead of you, Crater. I prefer they not know we're down here until we've made the calls."

Madison opened her basket and placed the silver piece in her dive pack. She let the basket float to the floor, since it was obvious their collection time was over.

"Don't lose your notes, but make sure you tuck them inside your wetsuits, out of sight. Store your cameras securely and try to hide them, if you can."

Ned and T.J. began the ascent. On their way, they

heard Wilson confirm he'd launched the bird, sending photographs downloading to his laptop. At the same time, he'd rigged it to send off a distress signal, which would be picked up by any civil defense, law enforcement, or coast guard receiver within a ten-mile radius.

"Good thinking, Wilson. Glad you're with us. T.J. and I are on our way. If you don't mind, Madison, you and Liz come up last."

"Got it," Liz acknowledged.

Ned climbed onto the deck at the stern, making as little splash as he could manage, and then helped T.J. with his equipment. He stored the detector in one of the compartments under the rear seating.

As others followed suit behind him, Ned watched their audience, who had not approached, regardless of what Lucas had claimed. The sleek yacht the group was using wasn't the same vessel they'd seen yesterday, but this one was even nicer, slightly larger and more modern. It looked brand new.

Wilson approached with his controller and asked for Ned's email to send images to. Ned also gave him the FBI contact information he'd been given over the phone. There wasn't any way they could send an explanation, but he hoped the pictures themselves would flag someone.

As Liz and Madison surfaced and stowed their equipment, three additional yachts appeared from the north, including the large black one reported stolen from the Bahamas.

He leaned over and whispered to Wilson, "Get that one, quick."

He watched as the screen showed the drone's call signs and even got a closeup of the occupants standing on the bridge. One was a woman.

"My com still working? Just nod your head if you can still hear me?" Ned watched as everyone acknowledged. "We're gonna get out of Dodge, just turn around and leave quietly without a confrontation. If they come after us, we'll keep moving east toward the shore. Danny, if it becomes a chase, you split off if you feel comfortable.

"Roger that."

"Gentlemen. Start your engines."

Wilson said something over the com to his cousin as a farewell in Navajo, Ned guessed.

It hit him right in the pit of his stomach. He was responsible for these good men. He prayed they could get back without incident.

As the four crafts began to follow, Wilson sped up. The Bones couldn't keep up their pace and began to drift back. As the cousins turned and waved to each other, Danny swerved off to the side and headed for a small sandbar off in the distance. He wouldn't be able to outrun them to shore, but he could make it to the sandbar before they were forced to slow down to keep from running aground.

Madison pressed her palm against Ned's back as they all watched one vehicle follow Danny, but the other three were closing in on the Lucky Strike.

"Ned, you take the wheel. I must bring in my drone."

"Can it follow?" Ned asked.

"It has time, but I'm getting ahead of its range. She'll drop from the sky if that happens.

Tucker barked an answer. "Send her over to Danny. You can crash her there on that island."

"Now that's a clever thought," Wilson said, adjusting the controls and then pushing the little craft in Danny's direction. Seconds after the bird disappeared from view, there was a large explosion and fireball from the direction of the sandbar as Ned and the rest of the team watched the Bones shatter into a million chards of light.

CHAPTER 16

"**D**ANNY!" WILSON YELLED.

Without asking, he circled back to head toward the island. The boat careened, nearly ending on its side, but successfully made the turn. Madison and everyone up top hung on to anything they could to avoid being tossed overboard. Liz fell on top of Andy and Jason. They all heard the sounds of pans and dishes and even humans being tossed about the small galley space below. Serena let out a scream and then cursed at the top of her lungs.

Ned was down the stairway, followed by Jake and Andy, helping Zak and the ladies recover from the disaster.

Wilson had clenched his jaw, bent over, and punched the power, determined to get to Danny.

Crater jumped to the bridge and tried to grab the wheel from Wilson's hands. As the two struggled, Crater yelled, "You turn around. You can't do anything for him. We *have* to get to shore. You don't want to mess with these people!"

Tucker Hudson, in one long leap, reached the bridge and picked Crater up. He was going to toss him overboard when Jason and T.J. stopped him.

"You fuckin' traitor!" Tucker said as he extricated himself from his buddies. The dive shop owner had been dumped on his ass, sprawling down the steps and onto the upper deck. Tucker was preparing to back it up with some serious physical pain for the man everyone now suspected of sabotaging their mission.

Ned's shirt was bloody when he popped up from the galley, but he otherwise seemed unhurt. "Tucker! Knock it off. He'll get his due."

"You want me to cuff him?" asked Damon. "I got zip ties."

"Get them," Ned shouted over the noise of the motor and the boat slicing through the waters of the Gulf.

Ned stared down at Crater, in total shock. "You knew about all this? How could you do this, Crater?"

The man's bloody lip upturned as he hung his head. He accepted the ties, placing his wrists together and allowing Damon to lash him to one of the chairs bolted to the decking. "No one was supposed to get hurt, okay? They were just supposed to scare you off."

"And then take our finds. That's fuckin' stealing," said Ned.

"Stupid Noonan. He was warned. You can't stand up to these guys."

"So now it's Noonan's fault?" Liz's voice was shrill. She held a pan, her elbow bloodied, looking like she was going to smash Crater's head in. "What a coward. You're a despicable human being."

Wilson kept hard charging until, all of a sudden, they ran right over their own debris field. Bits of fiberglass were flying through the late morning air. But there was no sign of Danny.

Madison looked behind them. One boat remained headed in their direction, but the other three were turning away. Ned focused on the beach, looking for Danny, when she grabbed his hand. "They're turning back. Ned, they're not coming after us. Just one boat—"

Wilson took a hard right turn to avoid hitting Danny, who was floating in the water face down. Madison lost her footing and fell overboard.

The water was warm, and for a split second, she forgot that she was in the middle of a chase, that Danny was perhaps badly injured or worse, and they were being pursued by a boatload of drug smugglers or pirates. Sounds of a motor became louder, and it was then she noticed the sleek black boat headed straight for her.

She paddled, trying desperately to get out of the way, but she knew she wasn't going to be fast enough.

There was no possibility she could do anything to stop the yacht from running her over, and the captain didn't have nearly enough time to stop. In a slow-motion dream-like trance, she braced herself for the pain of metal blades slicing through her flesh and did the only thing she could think of.

She dove down deep into the water. Hoping to God she was fast enough, she kept pushing with downward strokes, anticipating losing one or both legs, or perhaps just a foot at the ankle. Her imagination ran wild as any minute now her body was going to be in excruciating, horrible pain. She hoped it was followed by a quick death, not torn apart and still alive to feel every bite as sharks devoured her body.

And there it was, that pressure on her ankle, just one ankle. Her right ankle. But it wasn't a shark bite. It was someone's hand, grabbing hold of her leg and pulling her up. Did this mean her head was now in the path of the engine? So maybe this was better. Get it over with. No lingering agonizing death. She screamed until she realized she was completely out of breath.

Up out of the water, she was dragged. She kicked, trying to dive back in, but even though she thrashed, gulped in air and screamed, scratched and pushed, rolled over and over like a fish, she was restrained. Someone pulled her thigh, hand over hand. Then the top of her wet suit, pulling her, sliding her across the deck of the boat.

"No!" she continued to scream and felt her heel land in the soft flesh of someone's face. She kicked again, and this time felt warm liquid, blood, coming from the face of her attacker.

Another set of hands was on her body now, and she couldn't kick. A large body, a man's body had covered hers, immobilizing her, making it impossible for her to fight. They restrained her hands next.

Then someone said, "Madison, Goddammit. Stop fighting me. You're hurting me!"

Ned?

His face was bloody. His left eye was swelling, reaching the size of a hardboiled egg. His lip was split and draining red phlegm. His blue shirt was stained red and pink. He was trying to say something, but he was breathing so hard, he couldn't get a word out.

"Oh, Ned. Did they hurt you too?" she screamed.

Someone laughed in the distance. Ned gasped and started to choke, laughing. He spit out blood and gave her a smile through the wounds in his face.

"No, honey. But you did, Madison. You hurt me. You have a wicked, wicked kick. Beautiful legs, lovely to look at, but bad all the way to the bone. I just never knew how much I loved you until just now."

He fell back, laughing. Several other people stood over her, also smiling or chuckling. Someone gave her a cool towel. She righted herself, looking at all the blood spread over the deck, making it slippery. But she persisted, sitting up and placing the cool towel against his eye.

"I'm so sorry, Ned. I thought—"

"It doesn't matter Madison. We're okay. The cavalry has arrived, and we're safe."

"Danny?"

"Knocked out of breath, maybe a broken rib. Just guessing. But he'll be fine."

"How did you stop the boat?"

He laughed again, his elbow slipping on his own blood until he fell back against the deck again and let himself laugh more.

"It doesn't matter. It would take too long, and I don't have the energy."

"But—"

"Madison, just stop. Stop asking questions. Everyone's safe, and we got some of the bad guys anyway."

"Who's we?"

"Oh God, Madison. The Coasties. The ones you think look so sexy in their uniforms?"

"I did not say that."

"Oh, yes, you did. In your sleep, you've said it many times. I remember, because I don't wear a uniform, unless it's something official. But you like uniforms, don't you?" He gave her a smirk.

When she couldn't think of anything to say, she asked another question. "But how did you—?"

"If you don't stop with the questions, I'm not going to ask you to marry me."

Behind her, she heard clapping and a couple cheers. But his words got her attention. She wasn't going to say another word.

CHAPTER 17

THEIR DREAMS OF ending up rich and famous went up in smoke, just like the Barry Bones. Ned did feel badly about that but convinced himself it was Danny's fault, not his. That didn't make a bit of difference to Noonan, who could barely speak to him. His favorite words were, "What in the world were you thinking, going after all that shit without me?"

And even if he'd been tired of saying, "You were hooked up in the hospital after having your chest cracked," it would continue to do no good. Noonan was grieving, not about the treasure that wasn't there, but about the old Bones. He walked around the Salty Dog, down the street, over at the office they were shutting down across the street from the club. His maps and logs were gone. Noonan said he felt like he'd died that day in the water, so much of his past was lost.

The Salty Dog was the only place to meet him. It was where the conversations were too loud, the music even louder, and as the evening wore on, no one was making any sense talking to anyone. You could be with a person all night long and not remember a thing either of you said.

Noonan had been so convinced of the existence of this ship with the golden or silver mast he was willing to risk it all to see if it was there. And he very nearly did risk it all. He'd kept the threats on his life, on their lives, away from them so he didn't have to feel the rejection when they told him no.

But that would have been the right answer, he told Ned. If someone had said "No" sooner, Noonan would still have that ship. He could still pretend he was a pirate, full of adventure. He could still pretend that, if he could just lay his hands on the wheel of the Bones one more time, he'd find it. Find enough to put him in the lap of luxury, not smelling of fish and beer, sitting with his buddies, all jockeying for position to avoid picking up the tab.

"Well, we did get something out of it, Noonan."

"Not much. That wasn't my fault, either."

"No, it's never your fault, Noonan. But we did get the insurance finder's fee."

"You watch. They'll find a way to wiggle out of that too. You want to bet how much it will be?" he asked Ned.

"Sure. What are you willing to lose?"

He pulled out the dog collar that Otis had worn at one time—the first one, not the imitation, he was fond of saying. "I'll bet the whole farm there won't be more than twenty bucks."

"That's not fair, Noonan. Now you're just being a sour puss. Besides, I don't want that old thing."

Noonan put the collar back in his pocket. "It's hard when you're so old no one wants anything of yours. I remember when the ladies wanted all of me. Couldn't get enough of me, in fact. Beautiful ladies, like Amberley. Your father loved her too. You know that."

"Of course, I know that. You only tell me just about every day. So what are we going to bet, then? Let's make it realistic. A proper wager."

"Didn't you hear me? No one wants anything I've got, Ned. That's a problem."

"I know something you've got that I'd like to have."

"You don't say?" Noonan took another drag on his beer. He watched Madison wipe down the bar with a dishrag. "You promised you'd marry her, Ned. You remember that?"

"Yes, I did. And I will."

"When? When your ship sails in? When you get that treasure I've been looking for my whole life?"

"I want to be worthy of who she is. I want to be the man she thinks I am. This mission we went on, I fell for it. You conned me, didn't you?"

"No. I believed in it all along. I honestly thought there was a wreck with a silver masthead, embellished door handles, silver-plated dishes, grates on the storage areas. Maybe the anchor! But it's there, somewhere."

"Ah, so then you're going to look for another crypt, right?"

Noonan nearly spit out his beer. "After the next hurricane. But anyway, we were going to make a wager. I couldn't take anything from you, but what is it that you want of mine?"

"Memories."

"Excuse me?"

"Memories. Of Jake, my dad. I want to know what he was like. What he was like when he was happy, because he was never happy around me. I was the reason he couldn't have the life he wanted to have, was supposed to have."

"Don't say that. He had your mother. And what a prize she is, too. You're lucky to have such a mother."

Ned fingered the droplets of condensation on his beer. He was apprehensive to ask the question he'd always wanted to ask Noonan. Now was the time to be the kind of man Madison wanted and thought him to be.

"Why, Noonan, didn't he show me his happy side? Why did I bring him so much pain? What did I do to deserve that?"

In spite of himself, he did feel that deep, deep pain in his heart for the father he never got to know.

"I don't know, Ned. He always told me such wonderful things about you. He loved you very much. He loved your mother too. What he was unhappy about was that he wasn't good enough for Amberley. He knew he didn't deserve her. And he knew he could make your mother happy by giving her you. It was just the best he could do."

"Let's have that bet, then. If we get less than $1000 on the finder fee, you win. If we get more, I win."

"And what do you want of mine?"

"I don't want that dog collar. I want you to tell me stories about my dad. I want you to tell me the stories he should have told me. You can do it for him, or do it for me, makes no difference. But I'd like the gift of those memories, something I can think about instead of that grey, stiff old buzzard I saw that last day before we put him in the ground."

Noonan flicked a tear from his right eye and cleared his throat. "Okay, fair is fair. And if I'm the winner, I get to be your best man, stand by you at your wedding day. I get to be old Jake for a day. How about that?"

NED WAS PREPARING to leave for San Diego. He'd told Madison just one more deployment and then he'd make a decision. She was okay with it being his choice. She understood that about him. But she told him she didn't want to move to California, because everything magical was in Florida. She never wanted to live far from the beach, the warm beach, and she never wanted to have to work so damned hard she'd not be able to enjoy it.

He was fine with that.

"When I get back, the first thing we'll do is plan the wedding. I want you to pick out all kinds of pictures of how you want it to look like. I want as big or as little a wedding as you want. I want you to think about where you want to go on our first night married. Because when I'm gone, I can't think about things like that, so you'll have to think about them for me, okay?"

"It's a deal."

The postman rang their doorbell and had a certified letter addressed to him. There was another one addressed to Madison. It was from the insurance adjuster.

He was going to receive one hundred thousand dollars. They were also giving fifty thousand dollars to everyone on that dive trip—all seventeen of them, including Madison and Noonan.

"Amazing. Looks like we got the treasure after all," he said to her, swinging her around as if they were on a dance floor. "But you know what's even better?"

She smiled. "Tell me. I'm dying to know!"

"I won the bet."

"Who did you bet?"

"Noonan."

"What did you win?"

Ned smoothed his thumbs over her lower lip, slipped his fingers behind her ears, and pulled her to him. "It means I get to hear all the stories about my dad."

"That's what you asked for?"

"Indeed, I did."

"Ned Silver, I think you're the most amazing man I've ever met."

Did you enjoy Love's Treasure? I hope you'll follow along in the whole Sunset SEALs series, with the stories of the four Navy SEALs who found Happily Ever After on the white sand beaches of the Florida Gulf Coast.

SEALed At Sunset

Second Chance SEAL

Treasure Island SEAL

Escape to Sunset

The House at Sunset Beach

Second Chance Reunion

Love's Treasure

Finding Home (releasing summer 2022)

All of these books are also on Audible, narrated by the amazing J.D. Hart.

But wait! Do you want more SEALs? Want to read about the original SEAL Brotherhood men, starting with Kyle Lansdowne, Cooper, and all the other 9 original stories that brought Sharon to the attention of military romance readers.

The book that launched it all is Accidental SEAL, Book 1

But if you already know you want to read them all, in order and with bonus material, you want to get

The Ultimate SEAL Collection #1

The Ultimate SEAL Collection #2

I guarantee your life will be forever changed with these beautiful stories about the healing power of love.

ABOUT THE AUTHOR

NYT and USA/Today Bestselling Author Sharon Hamilton's SEAL Brotherhood series have earned her author rankings of #1 in Romantic Suspense, Military Romance and Contemporary Romance. Her other *Brotherhood* stand-alone series are: Bad Boys of SEAL Team 3, Band of Bachelors, True Blue SEALs, Nashville SEALs, Bone Frog Brotherhood, Sunset SEALs, Bone Frog Bachelor Series and SEAL Brotherhood Legacy Series. She is a contributing author to the very popular Shadow SEALs multi-author series.

Her SEALs and former SEALs have invested in two wineries, a lavender farm and a brewery in Sonoma County, which have become part of the new stories. They also have expanded to include Veteran-benefit projects on the Florida Gulf Coast, as well as projects in Africa and the Maldives. One of the SEAL wives has even launched her own women's fiction series. But old characters, as well as children of these SEAL heroes keep returning to all the newer books.

Sharon also writes sexy paranormals in two series: Golden Vampires of Tuscany and The Guardians.

A lifelong organic vegetable and flower gardener,

Sharon and her husband lived for fifty years in the Wine Country of Northern California, where many of her stories take place. Recently, they have moved to the beautiful Gulf Coast of Florida, with stories of shipwrecks, the white sugar-sand beaches of Sunset, Treasure Island and Indian Rocks Beaches.

She loves hearing from fans through her website: authorsharonhamilton.com

Find out more about Sharon, her upcoming releases, appearances and news when you sign up for Sharon's newsletter.

Facebook:
facebook.com/SharonHamiltonAuthor

Twitter:
twitter.com/sharonlhamilton

Pinterest:
pinterest.com/AuthorSharonH

Amazon:
amazon.com/Sharon-Hamilton/e/B004FQQMAC

BookBub:
bookbub.com/authors/sharon-hamilton

Youtube:
youtube.com/channel/UCDInkxXFpXp_4Vnq08ZxMBQ

Soundcloud:
soundcloud.com/sharon-hamilton-1

Sharon Hamilton's Rockin' Romance Readers:
facebook.com/groups/sealteamromance

Sharon Hamilton's Goodreads Group:
goodreads.com/group/show/199125-sharon-hamilton-readers-group

Visit Sharon's Online Store:
sharon-hamilton-author.myshopify.com

Join Sharon's Review Teams:

eBook Reviews:
sharonhamiltonassistant@gmail.com

Audio Reviews:
sharonhamiltonassistant@gmail.com

Life *is one fool thing after another.*
Love *is two fool things after each other.*

REVIEWS

PRAISE FOR THE
GOLDEN VAMPIRES OF TUSCANY SERIES

"Well to say the least I was thoroughly surprise. I have read many Vampire books, from Ann Rice to Kym Grosso and few other Authors, so yes I do like Vampires, not the super scary ones from the old days, but the new ones are far more interesting far more human than one can remember. I found Honeymoon Bite a totally engrossing book, I was not able to put it down, page after page I found delight, love, understanding, well that is until the bad bad Vamp started being really bad. But seeing someone love another person so much that they would do anything to protect them, well that had me going, then well there was more and for a while I thought it was the end of a beautiful love story that spanned not only time but, spanned Italy and California. Won't divulge how it ended, but I did shed a few tears after screaming but Sharon Hamilton did not let me down, she took me on amazing trip that I loved, look forward to reading another Vampire book of hers."

"An excellent paranormal romance that was exciting,

romantic, entertaining and very satisfying to read. It had me anticipating what would happen next many times over, so much so I could not put it down and even finished it up in a day. The vampires in this book were different from your average vampire, but I enjoy different variations and changes to the same old stuff. It made for a more unpredictable read and more adventurous to explore! Vampire lovers, any paranormal readers and even those who love the romance genre will enjoy Honeymoon Bite."

"This is the first non-Seal book of this author's I have read and I loved it. There is a cast-like hierarchy in this vampire community with humans at the very bottom and Golden vampires at the top. Lionel is a dark vampire who are servants of the Goldens. Phoebe is a Golden who has not decided if she will remain human or accept the turning to become a vampire. Either way she and Lionel can never be together since it is forbidden.

I enjoyed this story and I am looking forward to the next installment."

"A hauntingly romantic read. Old love lost and new love found. Family, heart, intrigue and vampires. Grabbed my attention and couldn't put down. Would definitely recommend."

PRAISE FOR THE
SEAL BROTHERHOOD SERIES

"Fans of Navy SEAL romance, I found a new author to feed your addiction. Finely written and loaded delicious with moments, Sharon Hamilton's storytelling satisfies like a thick bar of chocolate." —Marliss Melton, bestselling author of the *Team Twelve* Navy SEALs series

"Sharon Hamilton does an EXCELLENT job of fitting all the characters into a brotherhood of SEALS that may not be real but sure makes you feel that you have entered the circle and security of their world. The stories intertwine with each book before…and each book after and THAT is what makes Sharon Hamilton's SEAL Brotherhood Series so very interesting. You won't want to put down ANY of her books and they will keep you reading into the night when you should be sleeping. Start with this book…and you will not want to stop until you've read the whole series and then…you will be waiting for Sharon to write the next one." (5 Star Review)

"Kyle and Christy explode all over the pages in this first book, *[Accidental SEAL],* in a whole new series of SEALs. If the twist and turns don't get your heart jumping, then maybe the suspense will. This is a must read for those that are looking for love and adventure with a little sloppy love thrown in for good measure." (5 Star Review)

PRAISE FOR THE
BAD BOYS OF SEAL TEAM 3 SERIES

"I love reading this series! Once you start these books, you can hardly put them down. The mix of romance and suspense keeps you turning the pages one right after another! Can't wait until the next book!" (5 Star Review)

"I love all of Sharon's Seal books, but *[SEAL's Code]* may just be her best to date. Danny and Luci's journey is filled with a wonderful insight into the Native American life. It is a love story that will fill you with warmth and contentment. You will enjoy Danny's journey to become a SEAL and his reasons for it. Good job Sharon!" (5 Star Review)

PRAISE FOR THE
BAND OF BACHELORS SERIES

"*[Lucas]* was the first book in the Band of Bachelors series and it was a phenomenal start. I loved how we got to see the other SEALs we all love and we got a look at Lucas and Marcy. They had an instant attraction, and their love was very intense. This book had it all, suspense, steamy romance, humor, everything you want in a riveting, outstanding read. I can't wait to read the next book in this series." (5 Star Review)

PRAISE FOR THE
TRUE BLUE SEALS SERIES

"Keep the tissues box nearby as you read *True Blue SEALs: Zak* by Sharon Hamilton. I imagine more than I wish to that the circumstances surrounding Zak and Amy are all too real for returning military personnel and their families. Ms. Hamilton has put us right in the middle of struggles and successes that these two high school sweethearts endure. I have read several of Sharon Hamilton's military romances but will say this is the most emotionally intense of the ones that I have read. This is a well-written, realistic story with authentic characters that will have you rooting for them and proud of those who serve to keep us safe. This is an author who writes amazing stories that you love and cry with the characters. Fans of Jessica Scott and Marliss Melton will want to add Sharon Hamilton to their list of realistic military romance writers." (5 Star Review)

"Dear FATHER IN HEAVEN,

If I may respectfully say so sometimes you are a strange God. Though you love all mankind,

It seems you have special predilections too.

You seem to love those men who can stand up alone who face impossible odds, Who challenge every bully and every tyrant ~

Those men who know the heat and loneliness of Calvary. Possibly you cherish men of this stamp because you recognize the mark of your only son in them.

Since this unique group of men known as the SEALs know Calvary and suffering, teach them now the mystery of the resurrection ~ that they are indestructible, that they will live forever because of their deep faith in you.

And when they do come to heaven, may I respectfully warn you, Dear Father, they also know how to celebrate. So please be ready for them when they insert under your pearly gates.

Bless them, their devoted Families and their Country on this glorious occasion.

We ask this through the merits of your Son, Christ Jesus the Lord, Amen."

By Reverend E.J. McMalhon S.J. LCDR, CHC, USN
Awards Ceremony SEAL Team One
1975 At NAB, Coronado

Made in the USA
Columbia, SC
28 May 2022